10

# Cellars' Market

To honour an old-established and exclusive firm of wine merchants, a select dinner is held at a prestigious London restaurant. But when a famous wine from the merchant's cellars is opened in the presence of the assembled connoisseurs, it is not what the label describes. Faced by a crisis of confidence in his firm, the Chairman turns to an old friend, Bart Fraser, a successful London solicitor until his life was shattered by a personal tragedy which has resulted in his expulsion from the partnership.

Bart nevertheless agrees to take his old friend's instructions. He soon discovers that he is investigating more than an act of spite; the wine business is big money and at issue is a multi-million-dollar fraud which stretches from France to the United States mainland and even to the outer Hawaiian island of Maui.

But who is behind it? In his search for the truth Bart Fraser, himself a Master of Wine, is helped — or is he? — by a pretty gossip-column journalist for whom life has always been champagne and fun. As the action moves swiftly from the traditional centres of Beaune and Bordeaux to the East and West Coasts of America, a cunning plot emerges in which, as Bart grimly discovers, human life is cheaper than the cheapest plonk.

# DOUGLAS STEWART

# **Cellars' Market**

COLLINS, 8 GRAFTON STREET, LONDON W1

William Collins Sons & Co. Ltd
London · Glasgow · Sydney · Auckland
Toronto · Johannesburg

First published 1983
© Douglas Stewart 1983

British Library Cataloguing in Publication Data

Stewart, Douglas
Cellars' Market. — (Crime Club).
I. Title
823′.914[F]          PR6069.T/

ISBN 0 00 231370 7

Photoset in Compugraphic Baskerville
by T. J. Press (Padstow) Ltd.
Printed in Great Britain by
William Collins Sons & Co. Ltd, Glasgow

This book would not have been possible without the co-operation, expertise and kindness of so many people who helped me during my research. In particular I would like to thank and mention J. Fairweather Walker, B.Sc.; Michael Broadbent, Director of Christie's; Bill Hair and Jack de Carteret of Eldridge Pope, Ltd.; Michael Cornish and Brendan Bernard; the Officers of the US Bureau of Alcohol, Tobacco and Firearms at Dallas and Atlanta; the Officers of the Wine Institute of California; the Officers of the International Trade Mart, New Orleans, and in particular V. Edward Olson; Barbara Page, Director of Public Relations, Hyatt Regency Group; Wayne Richardson, Esq., of ABA International, Honolulu; the Directors and Staff of Noble Denton & Associates, Ltd.; the Savannah Port Authority, Georgia, and the Director of US Customs, Charleston, South Carolina; Emma Boxhall and Catherine Harman; Benjamin Hill III, Attorney, of Florida.

Finally, for the unenviable task of coping with all the secretarial problems, including a Word Processor with a defective memory, I thank my wife Penny, who has given up so much of her time to my project. Man *can* conquer machines but, at times with the Word Processor, this seemed an uneven match. Ultimately, therefore, my dedication is to secretary and machine: Beauty and the Beast.

# LONDON

'We must expel him from the Partnership. What with rising overheads and a rent review next year, every square foot of space is vital.' David Bream spoke with the forceful authority of Senior Partner of Bream and Bream, Solicitors, of London, S.W.1. Yet, despite his apparent concern for the future, his physique, his bearing gave no hint of penury. Indeed, his prosperous, fifty-five-year-old stomach was uncomfortably jammed between Regency chair and table. The hang-dog jowls came from too many chauffeur-driven visits to Ascot, Epsom and Cheltenham, while his other partners were working. Had his tailor been less expensive, the grossness would have been indecent. Above all, the generous expanse of his frame contrasted sharply with his mean, narrow outlook, voiced in the most peremptory tone.

A dollop of cigar ash settled comfortably on his belly. He flicked it aside as casually as he was now proposing to dispose of a partner. He stared at his three colleagues, each in turn. 'Bart Fraser must go. He hasn't earned his keep for months and I've got just the right man to replace him in the Partnership.'

Rupert Anderson, an ex-Navy man, was always quick to fall in line behind his Senior Partner. 'You've persuaded me. Never did like the cut of his jib. Too clever by half. Riding for a fall and all that sort of thing.' The faraway look in his eyes showed that his brain was as empty as the Atlantic, which he used to patrol. Regrettably, it was not as deep.

'A bit hard on Bart, yet you've persuaded me too,' said Bernard Salken, whose good sense and judgment were too frequently clouded by the material rewards for which he craved. Of all the partners, he was the most uncomfortable that the discussion was taking place in the absence of their partner, who was too unwell to attend. But the millstone mortgage, the commitment to his top-hat pension scheme and the lovingly polished Mercedes in Surrey, spoke louder than conscience.

Rolf Stein looked at those around him. Having been admitted as Junior Partner only seven weeks before, he was not expected to say anything and, as it was easier to say nothing, he contented himself with a nod of the head. David Bream was quick to notice such a nod when it suited him.

'Then we are all agreed,' he said. 'Bernard, I leave it to you to sort out the formalities. Make sure that Bart gets a letter in tomorrow morning's post.'

'You don't think we ought to talk to him? Get his viewpoint?' Bernard Salken looked somewhat sheepish at the task which had befallen him but he received no reply. For a second the chairman of the meeting looked at him, then simply turned away.

'The meeting is closed, gentlemen.' He rose from his chair and, pigeon-toed, shuffled silently over the thick carpet. The painting of his late father looked down, smug and complacent like his son. In the distance Big Ben struck eleven. Bream decided that it was time for a glass of malt in the privacy of his own room and then down to the Club for lunch.

The following morning, just across St James's Park, on the fourteenth floor of Stage House, the postman pushed the neatly typed envelope through the door of Bartholomew Fraser's luxury flat. It was Saturday morning and the heavy silence was broken only by the click of the letterbox as it snapped shut.

The flat enjoyed panoramic views to the south, taking in the sweeping curve of the Thames at Vauxhall, the

Crystal Palace mast and the endless nonentity of Battersea and Clapham. A chic address, suitable for Fraser's wealth, an address where money was assumed, where residents came and went with infinite regularity, their destinations Antibes, Geneva or New York. A second cousin to the Queen lived down the corridor, though Bartholomew Fraser was not interested, having chosen the flat as a contrast to his past and when his need had been urgent. There he'd hoped to rebuild his future — but it hadn't worked.

The small kitchen was clean and obviously unused. Across the corridor, the lounge-diner was dark, with heavy floor-length curtains shutting out the brightness of the morning. The furnishings were all starkly modern, from the black and red ottoman to the perspex display case and the tungsten spotlights clamped to the heavily patterned walls. Everything had been personally selected by the solicitor but he liked none of it and never had.

The bedroom too had been designed to his own specification, with deep green walls and matching carpet. The cover on the bed was lighter and everything had been blended carefully to the ultimate in modern perfection by interior decorators in Sloane Street. He loathed it.

There was another room into which Fraser would go every evening, staying there for perhaps ten minutes, sometimes longer. Then he would withdraw, lock the door behind him and go to the drinks cabinet to pour a generous Scotch into a Dartington tumbler. If he were not going out, Fraser would stand at the window, watching darkness fall over South London, watching the kaleidoscope of lights, or he would pace about, dragging his left leg behind him. Occasionally he would sit for a moment but then be on the move once again, occasionally replenishing the glass.

At bedtime, just as the evening before, he would take a couple of pain-killers and, with the whisky base, the agony of the shattered leg would be eased and the memories of the past would be blurred. Sometimes, as the black mantle of sleep descended, he almost felt equipped for a better tomorrow, for a fresh start, but by morning the pains had returned and the resolution had evaporated. On weekdays the prospect of getting out of bed to face another day at a desk was increasingly unthinkable. By ten o'clock, his leg would be throbbing and without fistfuls of pain-killers he'd never make lunchtime at all. But the alternative was amputation. The surgeon had made this plain. 'Endure the pain and hope for improvement in medical science. Better that than amputate now and medical science catch up just after.'

Fraser had heard the click of the letter-box from where he lay, debating what to do over the weekend ahead. The arrival of the post was the first noise that morning and gave him the incentive to force himself to stand, slightly twisted in his posture and unsure in his balance. As he stood naked beside the bed, his physique was that of a young man gone over-rapidly to seed, with his leg a patchwork of scarring criss-crossing the outer aspect of his thigh.

'Sod!' he exclaimed, as he struggled with his balance before moving into the hallway. It was hard to reconcile the crumpled figure with the young man who had got an Oxford Blue for rowing and squash twelve years before, when aged twenty-two. A mere two years before, he had been regarded as one of the toughest, most hard-talking young lawyers in London, but a lot can happen in two years and, in the case of Bart Fraser, a split second of fate had wound back the clock of his progress.

The letter seemed a long way down from his six-foottwo height and yet, despite the flab of wasted muscles, he remained a strong, fine-looking man. But what had been thirteen stone ten of hard packed muscle was now nearly fifteen stone of flabby indolence.

He tried to bend but it was too early in the day, so he showered and shaved, staring moodily into the mirror, hoping to find some flicker of steel to give him the courage to rebuild a better future. But nothing was different. Oh for the private ward, for the devoted care and that comforting hospital routine where kindness cocooned his inner fears. But then had come the discharge with a final 'Goodbye. Yes. I'll be all right. Thanks for everything.' A peck on the cheek for the nurse and he was alone in the bustle of Marylebone.

For want of anywhere better to go, he'd gone back to Forest Row, deep in the heart of rural Sussex.

He towelled his face dry and looked at it again, wondering which side of his face reflected what he had been and which side reflected what he would become. Either way, the truth was unpalatable. At Forest Row he remembered stopping in the gravelled drive, appreciating the five acres of lawn which sprawled in front of the sixteenth-century manor house with its mullioned windows and reassuringly solid front door.

Friends had offered to accompany him home that evening, but while appreciating their thoughtfulness he had declined. It was a time to be alone, a time to face his past and what he had done.

He could remember every movement, every moment, every rustle, every smell of that evening, as he had paused at the stone bench where *they* used to sit. He could recall making his way to the front door, haltingly and still with the stick which the hospital had provided. The key in the lock had been turned to the chorus of birds from the firs and the fruit trees and from the distant oaks. Somewhere a tractor had been bringing in hay. But inside, behind the heavy door, there had been not a sound. For a stupid, fleeting second he'd half expected the quick, running footsteps of a scampering child, had almost felt the little arms clasped round his leg in greeting. But no. There had been nothing except the serene timelessness of a manor house which stood impervious to the frailty of its occupants.

Seven months in hospital . . . but nothing had changed. Mrs Vernon had kept the place clean and tidy, just as she'd always done. Every book in his study was dusted and orderly; every cushion in the lounge was in place and puffed up to await the owner's return. The room still smelt faintly of apple logs and winter nights.

In the kitchen, he'd almost expected the smell of cooking, the clutter of Cordon Bleu graciousness. But it too was empty, quiet and respectful, dying of disuse-atrophy, like the walk-in temperature-controlled wine cellar. Rows of bottles lay untouched and undusted, for Mrs Vernon knew better. Every bottle had been selected with care and without regard to cost. From the pride of place 1945 Château Lafite, through the 1961's to the 1975's, every bottle had held great hopes for the future.

But there was a gap left by the bottle of 1961 Château Margaux. He'd opened and decanted it last thing before *that* journey. Laurel had been in the kitchen, putting the finishing touches to the dinner. And little Katy had been packing for her stay with Grandma. And so they had set out, just the three of them, in his Jensen. He'd known the road well, almost too well, and the car had loved the winding lanes, until the black ice sent it crunching deafeningly into a line of trees. And only he, he whose bloody fault it had been, had survived. A mile back down the road, the Château Margaux had come up to room temperature.

Now, as he combed his sandy hair in Stage House, he was no longer in the steamy, modern bathroom, but in the coolness of the old wine cellar at Forest Row. Though his income as a solicitor had been substantial, reflecting his ability, nevertheless the house had come from Laurel's side of the family and, being jointly owned, had passed to him, on her death, as survivor. One or two of her relatives, her sister in particular, had been somewhat unkind about 'Barty's £300,000 windfall' and, though never said to his face, the stories still reached him. And they had hurt. He cast the thoughts aside, trying to make plans for the day ahead. Perhaps a pub lunch and then a film. In aged jeans and black roll-neck pullover he returned to the hall and was pleased that he was able to pick up the letter at the third attempt. He wasn't particularly expecting anything and, with only passing interest, he removed the contents and was astounded to find the headed notepaper of Bream and Bream, his own firm, facing him.

Addressed to 'Dear Bartholomew', an instant omen, it was short, easily read, and its message was plain. The partners, after all due debate and consideration, had decided to expel him from the Partnership as, consequent upon his accident, he was unable to devote himself sufficiently to the firm. He was referred to Clause 28 of the Partnership Agreement.

He stared as the letter trembled in his hand. It was unbelievable, for surely he'd given good service, was *still* doing his best, despite his disability. Hadn't he arrived for work on time? Hadn't he fought to get through the day with the help of the pain-killers? There had just been that once. But surely that hadn't been serious? I mean, it wasn't as if I'd raped the typists or stolen the clients' money. Just a drink or two at lunch-time and a pain-killer, coupled with forty winks just before David Bream had arrived to introduce a new client. That was all. But then Bream had never taken kindly to the publicity after the accident; to the prosecution of his partner; to the regular absences to attend hospital for treatment.

'Bastards, selfish bastards,' he muttered as he walked to the panoramic window and stared into the distance. Come Monday morning—no office, no walk across the

Park. Nothing but thirty years of working life ahead with
nowhere to go and a gammy leg to get there.
Imperceptibly he found himself tramlining his way to the
drinks cupboard, but when he reached it something
stopped him, his hand on the doorknob. Indecision
showed on his face as the see-saw of attraction and
resistence raged in a battle which had been fought on
more than one occasion recently. Attraction had usually
won. But not this morning. He left the door closed,
searching instead in his pocket for the key to the door of
the spare-room.

It felt strange, standing in there on the bare lino with
the sun shining in. The large room seemed even larger,
due to lack of curtains and, indeed, a lack of all furniture
whatsoever. Yet the room was not empty. On the wall was
a photograph of Laurel, the one used by *Country Life*
when their engagement had been announced. At the time
she had been a leading model and their friendship had
filled the gossip columns for weeks. Further to the left was
one of Katy, little Katy with the beaming smile and
cascading fair hair, just as she had sat on her second
birthday. Between the photographs was a cheap
calendar, torn off to the 10th January, which had been
the date of the accident. And these were the last
remaining mementos of the past, the last remnants of
seven years of marriage. The most personal items had
been destroyed, the furniture from Sussex had been sold
at auction and the present flat selected and furnished in
total contrast to the perfection of the life-style which
they'd established, looking out across the Ashdown
Forest. With no cellar at Stage House, he'd agonized
about his wine and would have sold it, but his old friend
and wine merchant, Giles le Breton, had agreed to store it
free of charge 'till you get yourself sorted out, old chap'.

As the morning sun slanted through the window, the
radiant, matching features of mother and daughter

seemed to dance. Normally Bart Fraser would have stood there in silent remembrance, hurting himself, blaming himself, torturing himself for what he'd done. But not today, not this morning. With a single anguished yelp, he removed each picture and the calendar from the wall and, almost feverishly, tore the calendar into quarters, into eighths, into sixteenths, into thousandths, until all that remained was a small pile of paper on the floor. Fraser's strong features, with angular chin set defiantly, surveyed the bare wall, before leaving the room to place the photos in a drawer. Suddenly he felt unburdened, as if the shadows of the past were truly gone, as if he had consent from Laurel to rebuild something with the remains of his life, consent to cast aside the obsessional shrine and self-flagellation.

As he fed the pain-killers into the waste disposal unit, he was tempted to send Bream's letter the same way but he resisted. Cup of coffee in hand, he sipped reflectively. Every day is Saturday now, he told himself, so what to do? Well . . . he was still a solicitor, for the Law Society had not taken away his dog licence, his licence to bark as a solicitor. He was under a covenant from the partners not to compete with their business on termination of the Partnership but the clause was probably invalid if the reason for the dismissal were unfair. So he could compete. Huh! As if anyone wanted to consult him.

What's more it was about time that he found a girl-friend. Girl-friend? At his age? A Woman more like it. And not one that you had to pay. Especially not like Rachel hired for the evening from the Susannah Agency. £75 it had cost him but his limp performance had been laughable. No. Worse than that, for Rachel had actually laughed. But not before she'd taken his money from the non-event. Memories had been the bromide, had cast a mocking shadow over his pointless gyrations. He'd have to do better than that.

Anything else? Yes. He'd have to lose some weight. Get back his fitness. 'Do it now,' he told himself as he looked in the Yellow Pages for the address of the nearest gymnasium.


# PARIS

On the same morning as the Partners' Meeting in London, a small van laden with cases of expensive wine left its warehouse to join the blaring horns and ulcerating conditions of the Boulevard Périphérique. Switching from lane to lane with familiar ease, the driver took the exit at Porte Maillot, heading through the wet, cobbled streets until he reached the Rue de Longchamp, not far from the fashionable Avenue Foch and a mere mile from the Arc de Triomphe.

The driver, Claude Dupont, aged twenty-two, had worked for his present employers for eighteen months, delivering wine to the restaurants of Paris. If the job were undemanding, then it suited him, for he was unambitious and enjoyed the freedom to pace himself during the day, stopping off here for a beer, there for a coffee. With his wife of six months, he lived in a tall, unremarkable tower block in Courbevoie, where life was uncomplicated and humdrum, except on those occasions when he would bring home an expensive bottle of wine, which his employers believed had been broken in transit. The couple enjoyed those evenings, were delighted to make the break from the cheap five-franc Vin Ordinaire.

Dupont didn't regard himself as dishonest. It was just that, seeing the remarkable prices paid by the fat and the rich, he rationalized the occasional taste of the good life for himself.

A week previously a stranger had approached him in

the Café de la Paix near his place of work and, after a couple of beers, he'd been receptive to the man's chat, which had led to the promise of francs in the back pocket for a little job. No skill was required, no risk—just park his laden van in the second courtyard on the left, on the Rue de Longchamp. There was a café opposite, where he could dunk a croissant. After half an hour he had to drive to the Rue Benjamin Godard and call at the office of Pascal Schubert, where he would receive F. 1,000 for his trouble.

'And if my van isn't there?'

The stranger, whose accent had the lilt of the South, laughed. 'It will be there.'

'And when do I do this?'

'Next Friday morning.'

He knew the area well for this was the fashionable 16th Arrondissement and he parked in the yard after driving under the arch of a house. In the street there were quite a few people about but of the stranger there was not a sign. Doing exactly as he was told, he entered the steamy heat of the café and stood at the counter, glancing at his crumpled newspaper, his mind on what was happening elsewhere.

Back outside, the morning drizzle had turned to rain and his black hair was quickly dampened as, with racing heart, he returned, fully expecting to find the vehicle gone. But it was still there, exactly as he'd left it. He swung open the rear doors, expecting to see nothing but the space where the cases of wine had been stacked, but it was all still there, all F. 500,000 worth. Puzzled as to what had gone wrong, he climbed into his van and found a scrap of paper fixed to the steering-wheel. In clear, pencilled writing he read it. 'Take this note, not to the address given before, but to the house next door, on its left. Park opposite and bring this note with you. You must arrive before 9.00 a.m.'

Whistling to show his unconcern, he edged out of the courtyard into the busy street and reached the Rue Benjamin Godard in less than three minutes. He found the premises at once and knocked on the door of the five-storey terrace building.

'Ah! Monsieur Dupont.' The occupant was the man from the café, who took the piece of paper from him. Dupont was reassured to see the man and his face broke into a grin of satisfaction, born from his inner tension. 'Come in.' Dupont did so and the door shut behind him and he sensed an emptiness, a resonance from the tall dingy building. There was a lack of furniture, a lack of noise from the floors above. Of a concierge there was no sign.

'I did what I was told. Was it all right?'

'Yes. Perfect. Please follow me. You've done well.' His feet echoing from the flagged corridor, Dupont followed the quick-stepping man into another room which was barely lighter than the corridor. It too seemed to be empty, but no sooner was he through the door than someone unseen shut it behind him. With a slight gasp of surprise Dupont started to turn, but not enough to see the face of the burly man who had patiently awaited his arrival, a short rope held firmly in his hand. It was as well that Dupont had not seen the face, for it was strong, heartless and uninterested in the preservation of human life.

'*Mais* . . .' Dupont's sentence was strangled and, in the skilled hands of the killer, death came quickly. The man from the café looked on, interested only in the efficiency of the execution.

Dupont never did get the envelope.

His body was discovered in the empty building later that day. A restaurant proprietor who had been expecting a nine o'clock delivery had phoned Dupont's employers. He had received the usual excuses for lateness, but by midday the employers had told the police, who found the van where it had been parked and, under a seat, a bag full of transvestite magazines and ladies' underwear.

Supt. Jaubert and the gendarme checked the buildings nearby. '*Affreux!*' exclaimed the gendarme. In the centre of the empty room Dupont was hanging from a rope which passed over a hook in the ceiling, his body being counterbalanced by a concrete block on the other end. He was dressed in a red petticoat, with matching bra and panties underneath. Encircling the body on the floor was a selection of girlie magazines displaying female genitalia, and scribbled across the face of every girl in every photograph was the name 'Francette'.

Adhesive plaster gripped the mouth and his feet were padlocked together. Nearby lay his clothes and in a pocket. Jaubert found a key to the building, some small change and other inconsequential things.

The killers had done their job well, for next morning the serious papers gave the discovery of the body scant coverage. Sex and perversion of all types were rife in the 16th Arrondissement, but the popular press sensed a story and used titillating headlines like MARRIED MAN DIES IN SEX PERVERSION EPISODE and MASOCHISTIC SEX RITUAL ENDS IN DEATH. All the articles went on to explain that Jaubert was confident that the man had died accidentally during his own erotic exercises. The pornographic material found in the van was a useful pointer.

'This type of bondage is much more common than people realize,' said Jaubert at the press conference. 'Sometimes . . . it ends in death.' However, Mathilde Dupont, fifteen floors up in the greyness of Courbevoie, had more than the loss of her husband to bear as the gutter press hammered on her door, seeking a story and, where there was none, inventing and embellishing. That she denied knowledge of her husband's quirks made small news but the obsessional reference to Francette drove her frantic. Who was she? Where was she? How had her husband got to know her? What power had she over her husband that he should behave like this?

Nothing made sense and, with thirty press men crowding the staircase, baying for facts and photographs, she lay in bed sobbing, rejecting even the comfort of her mother.

That Claude Dupont had been murdered was never contemplated. The pathologist decided that death was due to vagal inhibition and probably took place, suddenly, without warning, while Dupont was enjoying himself in his own perverted manner. Within a week the story was dead and, one by one, the press slipped away, leaving only the widow to be concerned about the manner of her husband's death and the identity of the unknown Francette.

# LONDON

As quickly as he had made his decision to sell the Sussex manor house, Bart Fraser had left Stage House and moved to Belgravia Mews South. Expensive it might be, but £225,000 for immediate vacant possession seemed a small price to pay for the fresh start which he was making.

'Much improved, I think, Barty,' said the Hon. Giles le Breton as he sank into the deep velvet of the sofa. Giles had been at school with Fraser and was the only person who was permitted the licence of calling him Barty. He always had done and nothing was going to stop him now. 'I always hated that ottoman. Can't think what got into you, old chap — all those ghastly reds and blacks every-where. I thought you were quite off your rocker.'

Fraser laughed. 'I was.' He paused for a moment to sip a Bloody Mary. 'Or at least I was in danger of going mad when I was brought up with a jolt. I was living in the past . . . or trying to. Anyway, that's gone.' Fraser cast his eye around the comfortable drawing-room of the mews cottage. Its smallness gave an air of intimacy. 'Pills and booze, I'm afraid. But I'm through with it. The pills have gone.' Fraser lowered his eyes. 'Do you know, some days I got through the best part of a bottle of Scotch?' From the tone of voice Fraser was expecting a negative response.

'I know.' Giles's frankness was disarming and Fraser was shaken that the extent of his problems had been obvious because Giles, old friend that he was, had never passed adverse comment.

'God! Was it *that* obvious?' He didn't require an answer. 'Anyway, I'm much better. All I need is something to do. I've joined a health club in Jermyn Street. I go there every day. Circuit training for gammy legs.'

'No squat-thrusts?' laughed Giles.

'If I tried that, I'd break the other leg.' Fraser refilled Giles's glass. 'No. It's swimming mainly—lap after lap. Building up my muscles. After that I do a bit of leg raising and so on.'

Outside, in the cul-de-sac, the traditional street lamps cast a watery light over the narrowness of the mews. Fraser turned to his oldest friend, admiring the warmth of the man's personality, the kindness for which he was renowned. That he'd never married seemed to confirm the gentlest of rumours that he was homosexual, but it was an area about which Fraser preferred not to know. 'You're nervous?' he asked of his friend.

'About tonight, you mean?' Giles le Breton smiled reflectively. 'No, not at all.' Fraser was unsurprised at the answer, for Giles had all the poise and breeding which one would expect from someone of his background. A.H.

le Breton & Co., Ltd. had been wine shippers of St James's for over two hundred years and Giles was the latest in the family to have a controlling interest. Besides importing 'fine wines for the gentry', the family had farmed 1,500 acres of valuable pasture land near Winchester. If times had been hard, then the public would have gladly queued for a tour of the ancestral home, rich with its antiques and steeped in history. But times had never been hard.

'But a dinner in your honour, given by the Wine Writers' Association, celebrating two hundred years of your company, must mean a lot.'

'It does.' Giles pushed back his long fair hair with a languid sweep of an arm. It was a sign of embarrassment, a habit entirely in keeping with his self-effacement. 'Tonight must be the greatest accolade that I'm ever likely to achieve. Of course, I've been given all kinds of *personal* honours, such as becoming a Master of Wine like you. They were fun. But this is the most discerning recognition for my company.'

'Any jealousy from other shippers?'

'Good Lord, no! We compete only in providing the best quality at the right price. We're not . . . carbon paper salesmen. No, not at all, my dear Barty.' Fraser felt no embarrassment at the endearments which he knew Giles used as mere figures of speech.

'Time to go, I would think,' said Fraser, hearing a cab stop outside. The two men reached the door together. 'Giles—do me one favour. If you see me drinking too heavily, then you must say so.'

'You'll be all right. I'll see to that, Barty.' The affectionate arm across the shoulder spoke again of twenty years' friendship and not at all of impropriety. 'By the way, did you say you still haven't got a job?'

'No. I'm not really sure what I want.'

'But you'll remain a solicitor?'

'It's a good meal ticket. All I need are clients.' They climbed into the cab and soon it was speeding round Hyde Park Corner on its way to Southampton Street, W.C.2. 'You had plenty of clients at Bream and Bream, didn't you?'

'Yes. But they belong to Bream and Bream. Not to me.'

'Oh, come off it, Barty! Take me for example. I went to Bream and Bream because of you. Now that you've parted company, then I follow you, and there must be dozens like me.' Le Breton's smooth, oval face with its deep-set eyes showed both concern and sincerity.

'Thanks for saying so but I don't think Bream and his crew would see it that way. They'd probably take out an injuction to prevent me from competing or stealing their clients.'

'You wouldn't let *that* stand in your way, would you? I wouldn't give a toss for that lot, Barty. If you want to set up your own business, you do so.' Le Breton looked hard at his friend. 'You fight them if you have to. One day they'll realize what they've done. Biggest mistake they ever made.'

Bart gave a shy smile of the type which had been missing since that day in January. 'Maybe. I'm sure they can't expel me under the Partnership Deed but you know, Giles, in a funny sort of way I'm grateful to them. It was their letter which brought me to my senses. It was a watershed.' The taxi was still crawling through Trafalgar Square as he was speaking, neon lights shimmering off the backs of the lions at the foot of Nelson's Column. 'But God, how I miss Laurel! It's a different kind of hurt now, though. Less painful. More detached, more able to think back on the good times without guilt.'

Both men drifted into silence, each apparently watching the people thronging the Strand but Fraser's thoughts were locked in fragmented memories of the past. A nudge on his arm snapped him into the present. He looked out and saw the discreet sign of the famous restaurant selected by the Wine Writers' Association for the celebration.

L'Esprit de Bourgogne was now regarded as the leading restaurant in the West End, renowned particularly for its distinguished cellar. Inside, Giles le Breton and his guest were greeted with respectful nods and murmured 'good evenings', as the assembled company stood around opulently in the Edwardian excellence of the reception area. Someone unseen tried to start a round of applause in le Breton's honour but the rest of the company regarded this as premature and the noise died away. Among the welter of well-known faces, Bart Fraser picked out a dozen of the most finely tuned palates in the country. The air was charged with expectancy of a great occasion and, to Fraser, there seemed a touch too much reverence, a touch too little enjoyment.

Jean-Luc Pichet, the proprietor, came forward to shake hands with Giles le Breton. 'Monsieur Giles!, Monsieur Barth-ol-o-mew. It is good to see you.' Though the Frenchman had lived in England for twenty-five years, his English was spoken with the precision of a Frenchman still struggling with his first words. 'It is a great honour that my restaurant has been chosen for this important, very important occasion.'

'And very fitting, if I may say so,' said Giles, accepting a glass of dry sherry from a silver tray. 'Besides which, your restaurant is one of my firm's best customers.' The three men laughed.

'If you'll excuse me, Monsieur Giles, I must check the final arrangements. Everything, but everything, must be perfection tonight.'

The small man, who had spurned all personal relationships to nurture his restaurant, slipped away through the thirty or forty people in the ante-room. Le

Breton was quickly surrounded by a group of writers, including Marjorie Harley, who was Chairman of the Association.

Fraser excused himself and went over to the giant sideboard and mixed with the cluster of people studying the menu. There were eight courses, accompanied by Chablis 1971, Chambertin 1969, and concluding with Veuve Clicquot 1966.

'Excellent choice of wines,' said one.

'Perfect, to go with that magnificent menu,' replied another, adding 'and all, of course, shipped by A.H. le Breton & Co., aren't they?'

'Indeed yes,' replied the first. 'No problems tonight, but if we repeat this another year, that's when our difficulties will arise: when we have to select the wines of a less distinguished shipper. With any luck, I'll be off the Committee.'

It was at that precise moment that Monsieur Pichet returned with Giles and Marjorie Harley. The look of consternation on her face was shared by the tone of Giles's voice. 'Don't ask any questions. Just casually follow us.' The voice was low, yet urgent.

Trying to look natural, Fraser followed them from the bar, through the dining-room and into the kitchen, where there must have been eighteen people working under the chef in an atmosphere of clockwork efficiency. On they went into a side room where the sommelier, himself a Master of Wine, was standing alone, looking perplexed. It was his duty to provide wines, in a state of perfection, for every occasion and, in front of him, were the twenty bottles of Chambertin. The corks on each had been drawn and he had started to decant one of the bottles for tasting.

'You will not know my sommelier, Monsieur Blouson,' said Pichet. 'He is concerned about the quality of the wine.' The proprietor had his eyes down and the nervous movements of his hands and feet gave away his stress, his embarrassment at having to say this, not simply to a Guest of Honour, but to the man whose company had shipped the wine from France in the first place. It was a nightmare! It was a crisis for which his Gallic temperament was not equipped.

Quickly yet steadily, the sommelier poured each of those present a small quantity of the wine, each from a different bottle. In unison each raised a glass before tilting, sniffing, swirling, studying the colour, sensing the bouquet. Bart Fraser had been a Sunday newspaper's 'Wine Taster of the Year' and, in 1978, had passed the extensive examinations, including blind tastings, to become a member of the elite Institute of the Masters of Wine. As a member of this select and highly respected body, he knew at a glance that the wine was not Chambertin 1969. Chambertin, this King of Wines, thought by many to be the greatest Burgundy in the world, should have been the high point of the evening, but a glance had shown Fraser that the colour was too red, the bouquet too misleading, to have come from the narrow strip of Burgundy entitled to the classification of Chambertin.

It was Giles le Breton, with his infinite breeding, who broke everyone's embarrassment. 'I'm not sure what it is, but it's not Chambertin 1969. Come to that, it's not Chambertin of *any* year.'

The admission unleashed everyone's tongue. 'I'm sorry, Giles,' said Marjorie Harley, 'but I'm not even convinced that this comes from Burgundy at all. To me, the after-taste smacks of somewhere much further south — the Côtes de Roussillon, for example. What do you think?' She turned in the direction of Fraser.

'A few years ago I'd have said Algeria,' said Fraser, 'but I think that less likely now. I wouldn't argue with you but my guess is Italy.'

'*Mon Dieu!* What are we going to do? What are we going to do?' Pichet was in despair, as visions of disappearing Michelin Guide stars flashed before his eyes.

Le Breton's calmness was in contrast. 'Well, first we owe a vote of thanks to your sommelier, without whose skill we would all have been publicly humiliated.'

'But the menu! It says the wine will be Chambertin.'

'What I suggest you do,' said Fraser, 'is to tell the truth. But in a low-key way.' He looked at Marjorie, majestic Marjorie, in her expensive evening gown and built like a duchess. 'I'm sure you can say the right thing. Something on the lines of 'our Guest of Honour felt that one or two of the bottles weren't up to the Company's reputation for this occasion . . .'

'and he has invited everyone to enjoy a 1964 Nuits St Georges in its place.' It was Giles le Breton himself who finished the sentence. There was silence for a moment as everyone assimilated the position, each realizing that the integrity and reputation of Giles's company was at stake.

'If you say so, Monsieur Giles . . .'

'Of course I mean it, my friend. Get the wine up and opened urgently. Will the temperature be all right, Monsieur Blouson?'

The sommelier shrugged. 'I'll try.'

'Wait.' It was Fraser's voice, strong and assertive. 'Everyone here must say nothing of what has just passed. The full story must not come out and, from this moment on, everyone talks only of the Chambertin being "not up to standard". Agreed?'

At first everyone seemed to be nodding but then Marjorie Harley frowned. 'I'm concerned about my duty to the Association and to the public. This is a criminal matter.'

'My dear Marjorie,' said Giles, stretching out a languid arm and gently touching her elbow, 'the last thing I want is to embarrass you, worse still to compromise you. Rest assured, no expense will be spared to find out what has happened.'

Marjorie Harley bit her lower lip and her face showed that her conscience was being torn in half. 'I don't want you to take this wrongly, Giles, but I can't be a party to a cover up. Put it this way: I ordered these wines in good faith tonight. I now know that the Chambertin 1969, shipped by your company, is not what it seems. Put simply, it's plonk. Why it's plonk, or how it became plonk I know not. But do I not have a duty to reveal this to the public?'

'Of course you're right, Marjorie, and, if you feel you must speak out now, then I have no intention of stopping you. What I do ask you to consider is the number of reputations which will be smeared without justification. Even Monsieur Pichet and his restaurant will be looked at askance by doubting customers.'

Fraser, listening to the exchanges, still felt that Marjorie Harley looked tempted to take Giles's good nature at its word and to reveal everything. 'I've got another idea,' he intervened. 'I'm sure you don't believe that Giles would be a party to fraud. That . . . is quite unthinkable. Might I suggest that we have your word that you will say nothing for three months, to give Giles the chance to investigate. If the truth of the fraud can be discovered within that time, then no doubt he will welcome the exposure as much as you. If he cannot do so, then surely he cannot crave your indulgence any further.' Fraser enjoyed the freedom to speak, not as a solicitor but as a layman.

Marjorie was silent for an age. 'I agree.'

'And it will be for you, Monsieur Pichet, to ensure that your sommelier says nothing. The Chambertin must be returned to Giles tomorrow and his company must be permitted to take samples of any wines from your cellars without warning. You understand that, don't you?'

Pichet, still trembling, looked at Fraser and then at Giles to satisfy himself that the lawyer was talking with Giles's authority. 'All right. I go along with what you say. We at L'Esprit de Bourgogne, will not—how you say?—blow the gaff.'

It was nearly 2.00 a.m. when the taxi stopped outside Fraser's cottage at Belgravia Mews, its exterior highlighted by a cabby lamp above the door. The evening had gone well and in the first floor drawing-room, still smelling faintly of the cigars enjoyed before their departure, the mood was relaxed, bow ties unleashed, jackets flung over chairbacks. But the impact of the bogus wine was hitting Giles hard. Reality had to be faced. Someone had it in for him. Bottles, specially imported from trusted friends in Beaune, had been filled with dishonest wine. The thought made him shiver in the warmth of the room.

Fraser poured a large Armagnac for his friend and a smaller one for himself. Two weeks before he'd have slipped himself twice the amount and then some more on top. But he resisted.

Giles threw a shoe across the room and then swung a lazy leg over the end of the sofa. It was a move of deceptive casualness, for his mind was in a ferment. 'Barty, my dear chap, have you ever felt that someone really hated you? Have you ever felt that someone wanted to ruin your business, shatter your reputation?'

Fraser handed him the glass. 'It was a close thing. We were lucky, but you're convinced that someone's got it in for you?'

'Must have.' The over-simplicity of the answer matched the despairing voice, the defeated eyes and the pallor in Giles's normally slightly florid cheeks.

'Who, then?'

'God knows.'

'Perhaps they weren't after you. Perhaps it was the restaurant. Someone anxious to kill the restaurant's reputation?'

'No. I doubt it. You know as well as I do that the occasional bad bottle of wine is an everyday hazard. This was different. The whole lot . . . the whole bloody lot of the Chambertin was fraudulent. Can you believe it?'

'I've got to.' It was a silly response but said while Fraser was thinking of something else, thinking round the problem, trying to find a new perspective.

'If this gets out, mere protestations that my company are innocent will make no difference. Our reputation will be tarnished forever, until such time as I can show what happened.' He handed over the empty glass for re-charging. 'And so this must never come out, the truth of tonight must remain secret until we can tell the world who was responsible for what had occurred. But whoever did it must really hate me, hate everything for which I and my family have always stood.' Fraser nodded, leaving the various rhetorical questions unanswered.

'My company's name is probably the most copper-bottomed guarantee in the business. Even in 1973, after the Winegate scandal in Bordeaux, not one of our customers really suffered. At least, they didn't suffer in terms of quality, although some of the speculators may have got their fingers burned.' He turned to his solicitor. 'This could mean a prosecution, couldn't it? If it came out I mean?'

'It's possible. There are powers under the Trades Description Act but I think it unlikely and I don't regard that as your real problem.'

'Which is?'

'That the word should get out that your company's Chambertin 1969 is the sort of plonk which you would take to a party in Fulham, while hoping someone else has brought something better. Because of Marjorie Harley, you've only got a short time to get to the bottom of it. What you must do is check the history of the wine, starting in the restaurant, working back to your cellars, to shipment from Beaune, right back to the vineyard.'

'So you include my company in the suspicion?' Giles's voice was raised in disappointment and anger.

'I include everybody in this—everybody but you. I certainly do not rule out your company, for that is only as good as the least honest member of your staff. There may be someone on your staff with a grudge, a former member of your staff who has a vendetta for reasons good or imagined. It might even be a competitor, but more likely than not your answer lies in Beaune.'

'But our merchants, our négociants in Beaune, are of the highest repute.'

Fraser laughed. 'Giles! You always were too nice about people, always seeing the best, never believing the worst. And I doubt you'll ever change.' While he was talking Fraser's memories were of their schooldays together, of the artless, open boy who could never tell a lie. 'The people with whom *you* deal may be of the highest repute but they too are dependent on their staff. As a solicitor, I'm trained to be suspicious, to disbelieve, to turn situations upside down and inside out. Sometimes my suspicions have been so unfounded that I should have felt embarrassed at having even entertained them—but I never have.'

'You always were one to see Reds under the bed,' responded Giles, but not as a reprimand this time. 'Do you think Marjorie might give us a bit longer if we needed it?'

'Not at this stage. She's a tough old bird, full of exceedingly boring Christian virtues. But if you were on to something, then I might get her to agree to a bit longer.'

Giles stretched out of the chair to help himself to

another Armagnac. Even the way he walked now was different from before the dinner. The peacock strut had given way to the whipped dog sidle. When he returned, his face almost ashen in the half light of the smoky room, he spoke again. 'Well, you've got your first job. I can't cope with this.'

'You mean you're instructing me?'

'Exactly. You understand the wine trade backwards; you're my solicitor and I'm in legal trouble.'

'But what about Bream and Bream?'

'Don't worry about them. You help me. We'll worry about them later. From what you said, they're not worthy of any more thought.'

'I'll do it on one condition.'

'Being?'

'That we don't hide it from Bream and Bream. I won't have them deceived.'

'That's a deal then. You'll start work tomorrow.'

'And my brief?'

'To work day and night, go anywhere, do anything to beat the deadline. Any reasonable disbursements can be incurred. My company is, after all, "By Royal Appointment". God help me if that sort of rubbish reaches the Palace.'

'And there's me trying to cut back on drink and my first job is swigging wine to see if it's genuine.'

Giles came towards him, put his glass on the inlaid coffee table and, in a gesture of solidarity, placed a hand on each of Fraser's shoulders. It was obvious that Giles was fighting back tears. 'Don't let me down. You remember what happened to Hermann Cruse in the Winegate scandal? Of course you do.'

'Yes.' Fraser's response, short though it was, was long drawn out, as he realized of what Giles was thinking. Hermann Cruse, a leading wine figure in Bordeaux, had been unable to face the wine scandal surrounding his family and had committed suicide by jumping into the River Gironde. 'Yes. Yes, I remember only too well.'

The implication hung heavily in the air as the two men said goodnight.


# NEW ORLEANS

About a week before Giles and Barty had listened to the speeches at L'Esprit de Bourgogne, a well-dressed couple had been walking down noisy Bourbon Street. Hubert Zeeler was forty-two, although he looked several years younger. His hair was generous both in length and quantity, but his face was hard, distant and unsmiling, with eyes hidden behind tinted glasses. The immaculate linen suit, carefully chosen for the sticky weather, emphasized his bearing, which was tall and commanding.

Annie Maguire, his companion, was twenty-nine, her brown hair tightly swept back on top of her head in a style which did nothing for her features, or perhaps did too much for them. Nevertheless, she still attracted a few casual glances, due to the figure-hugging pink outfit which she was wearing.

Bourbon Street, if it ever catered for couples, no longer did so. As a pair, they were too smart, too together for a street where jazz could be heard but less often seen amid surroundings of hookers, clip-joints and seedy bars, with blaring rock music. Yet the street retained a fascination, its style French, if one troubled to look beneath its gaudy make-up. Everywhere was noise, be it the sound of black voices raised in anger, or the sound of country music competing with shouted invitations to enjoy the delights of an Oriental Body Massage. Such jazz as still remained wouldn't flourish until later and the show at Al Hirt's Club wouldn't start for another two hours.

They turned into Toulouse and then again into Royal Street, where their well-dressed appearance was less obvious, their togetherness more in keeping. They were in no hurry, dawdling outside the antique shops, considering the price of gold, studying the fine wrought-iron balconies and the huge lights heavily suspended outside the premises of Royal & Co., Antiques. They could have been tourists, tasting the delights of the Vieux Carré, the pearl in the violent, throbbing oyster of New Orleans, but they were in fact working, having flown in earlier from New York. They had checked in at their hotel on Dauphine Street and were now ready to dine at Atkinson's, long acclaimed as the finest restaurant in the city. Unless one had enjoyed *both* breakfast and dinner on their patio, it was said that one had never visited New Orleans at all.

Zeeler was satisfied. Their table was centrally placed, close by the fountain in the courtyard, with forty or more diners scattered about them in groups. The gas lamps were straight from Jack the Ripper's London and cast pools of light across the pink tablecloths.

'Damn the rules,' said Zeeler, removing his jacket and hanging it across the back of his chair. The temperature was still hovering around the eighty mark and the humidity was higher than that. 'Kinda nice in here, huh?' It was barely a question, more of a grudging acknowledgement that their surroundings were something special.

'Sure!' Annie Maguire's voice was Brooklyn, hard, disinterested, laconic, sounding as though she were chewing gum. She continued to browse through the menu, tired of the way of life which Zeeler was leading now. But it would soon be over.

The waiter returned, briskly efficient. 'You-all ready to order?' he enquired, after putting down the drinks.

'Yuh! Two Crab and Shrimp au Gratin.' There was no

pretence at trying for the French accent. 'Then Rack of Lamb.'

'Would you-all like some wine, sir?' In Atkinson's — one drank wine. To say no would have been an affront.

'We'll have a bottle of the Château Plaisance 1966.' Zeeler's selection of a particularly good wine from the Margaux region of Bordeaux met with the waiter's nod of approval. Customers prepared to pay over a hundred dollars for a bottle of wine certainly knew what they wanted. But Zeeler had been briefed on the choice of wine, well briefed.

'Very good, sir. I'll have the wine waiter bring it right away.'

'Sure. Let it breathe a little.'

The couple chatted in low tones, admiring the subtle lighting which emphasized the lush greenery of the shrubs and trees which overhung the tables. From a distant bedroom came the sound of a youngster meddling with his father's trombone and from all around came the discreet chatter of contented people.

'Your wine, sir.' The wine waiter had arrived with a flourish and, after much displaying of the expensive label, drew the cork, sniffed and gave a slightly concerned look, but proceeded to pour a small amount into Zeeler's glass for him to taste.

As Zeeler did so, there was an instant look of disgust. Ostentatiously he spat out the wine on to the tiled floor. 'Jesus bloody Christ!' His voice was loud. 'More than a hundred lousy bucks a bottle!' His fist thumped the table, while the wine waiter, startled, took a step backwards, shaken at the reaction. 'If you-all wait a minute, sir . . .' He'd intended to say that he would try the wine himself but his hushed tone was shouted down.

'You tellin' me that's from France? Then I'm tellin' you, you goddamned bastard, that wine came straight from the Mississippi.' Zeeler was on his feet now, shouting like a man possessed, his arms outstretched, every eye in the room riveted upon him. 'You just go on ahead and taste that.' He grabbed the wine bottle from the waiter and poured another slurp into the glass. Shaken at what was happening, the wine waiter dithered, enabling Zeeler to continue with his outburst. 'Go on. Taste it. Where's the boss? Send for the Maître d'!' Every table had stopped eating, had stopped drinking and all eyes were on the two men. From the kitchen came both owner and Maître d'. 'Taste it! Taste it!' urged Zeeler. 'You the boss here? Then you taste this goddamned stuff too.' Carelessly he sloshed some more wine into another glass. 'Call that Château Plaisance 1966!' Zeeler started a tour round the tables, still clutching the bottle in one hand and pointed at the label in the other. 'Château Trashcan! That's what I call it. Chateau Trâshcan 1983!' His demonstration over, he returned to his own table, where the wine waiter and owner were conferring, nodding heads in agreement.

'I'm sorry, sir. This must be a bad bottle.' His next words were lost as Zeeler interrupted.

'That ain't no bad bottle. That's just bad wine. And that wine ain't been no nearer France than I have.' Zeeler nodded to Annie as he grabbed his jacket. 'Come on, honey, come on. We're taking this bottle straight to the cops.' He turned to the owner, who was at least a foot shorter than him. 'This some kinda clip joint?' As Annie rose her hand appeared to catch the tablecloth, causing cutlery, glassware and food to crash to the floor.

Ignoring the chaos, Zeeler grabbed her arm. 'Forget it, honey.' Clutching her arm, he led her towards the exit. There was a flash of a camera just catching a back view of the departing couple with the bottle clasped firmly in the man's hand.

The owner nearly followed but decided instead to build a few bridges with his remaining clientele. An uneasy silence filled the hot, damp air.

'I'm sorry about that. Some kind of nut. Over-reacted, I guess. I hope it won't spoil your evening with us. There'll be champagne cocktails for everybody.' The owner could think of nothing better and headed back to the kitchen.

'Ah just hope this champagne ain't goin' to be Château Garbage,' was a comment from somewhere.

Meanwhile the couple had moved quickly and were soon back in their hotel.

Next morning they took the eight o'clock flight to Atlanta to change planes for the long haul up to Seattle to repeat the charade. Annie handed him the local newspaper, which she'd just bought. 'Don't really look like you,' she said.

Zeeler took the paper. 'Nope. But then that guy was paid to take a back view. Let's see what they've written.' He read it out.

'Last night the tranquility of Atkinson's Restaurant was torn apart by a rich, well-dressed stranger, having a night on the town with his chick. The man, aged about thirty-five, having ordered wine costing over a hundred bucks a bottle, broke up the place, shouting that it tasted like the Mississippi. In the confusion, his table was overturned. One observer said that he threw a chair across the room.' Zeeler paused, laughing. 'That's not true but it's what it says. Anyway it goes on. "The stranger disappeared, taking away the bottle for analysis. A spokesman for the restaurant agreed that the wine was not up to standard but refused to make any other comment. Another diner, Richard Hoffmeyer III, told our reporter that he had been able to sneak a sip from the glass which the owner had tasted. He agreed that the wine was not Château Plaisance, commenting, 'I wouldn't give that stuff to a dying horse,' and adding that he was something of a connoisseur in these matters." '

'Dying horses or the wine?' Annie Maguire spat out her gum.

'It don't say. Hoffmeyer ordered a bottle for himself but the management refused to deal, so he wants the entire stocks of the restaurant checked by the Public Analyst.'

'That's a bonus.'

'And when I get this report back to New York with some of the others, I'm gonna get a bonus too.' He counted on one hand. 'Myrtle Beach, three weeks ago Tuesday. Chicago the week before that, last week Houston and San Francisco; tomorrow night Seattle and we've just struck the jackpot in New Orleans. Real soon someone's goin' to start askin' questions about this crap the French are sending us.'

## LONDON

Bartholomew Fraser heard the telephone ringing. He'd heard it before but had felt disinclined to get out of bed. His head was throbbing, his leg was pounding and his mouth was dry. The night had been too short and, even with the long lie-in, he felt little better. He'd managed to sleep but the alcohol and the parting conversation with Giles had guaranteed a disturbed night. Whether he'd been awake or asleep he was unclear, as dream and reality had blended into a nightmare of Hermann Cruse, or was it Giles, jumping from the Bridge.

Each ring of the phone was a reprimand for having drunk too much the night before, a reminder that he was not as far on the road to recovery as he'd thought.

He forced himself to the phone and it was a relief to have it silenced at last. 'Barty!' said Giles. 'Do you know what the time is? It's a quarter past two.' He answered his own question.

'Really.'

'For God's sake! You know it's urgent.'

'Sorry! I've let you down a bit. Had a bad night.'

'Barty! I thought you wouldn't let me down.' Giles was speaking from his home in St John's Wood, sitting at the neat, orderly desk with not a working paper in sight. He knew of the drink problem, probably better than anybody, but had felt that the corner had been turned. There had been no better commercial lawyer in London, tough both mentally and physically, a match for anybody. He remembered Fraser the daredevil, who had climbed down knotted sheets from the third-floor dormitory. He recalled the occasion at Hythe when Fraser had jumped into a wild, turbulent sea to rescue a toddler who had been swept from the promenade by a giant wave. He knew he couldn't have done it. But that was the difference between them. Typically too, Barty had left the scene a hero without leaving a name. But today? The voice at the other end of the phone sounded beaten and as despairing as he'd felt the night before. Lord love us, can I really rely on him now? 'I'm coming straight over,' Giles said. 'See you in twenty minutes.'

When le Breton arrived at the door Fraser had worked fast, showering quickly and putting on blue cord trousers and a clean check shirt. Only his eyes gave away the story of the night before.

'Can I get you a drink, Giles?'

'Have you left any?'

'Plenty of soft drinks, anyway,' Fraser laughed, breaking into a cough as he did so.

'If there were money back on empties, you'd be a rich man.' The banter then left Giles's voice as the moment of friendship changed into the moment of business. 'Barty: there can be no repetition of this.'

Fraser kept on the move. 'You're right. There won't be.

I hated seeing you so down and slipped myself the odd one or two after you'd gone.'

The wine shipper stooped to pick up the empty bottle of Armagnac. 'So I notice.'

'No, you've got to believe me, Giles.' Fraser's face was imploring. 'I'd grown cocky, believing I was cured, but last night shows that I've still got to be careful. It was as if I were throwing down the gauntlet for myself or playing Russian Roulette with all chambers loaded.'

Outside, a gentle rain was still falling on the cobbles and a passing cab made a pleasing hiss. The bright red painted door opposite gave him no cheer. 'But believe me — it wasn't the stress which broke me up. It wasn't my fear that I couldn't do the job. I *know* I can do it. If you take this job away from me, then every day will be an eternity, an opportunity for more loneliness and more self-analysis.' His face was imploring, crying out for understanding.

For a friend, Giles spoke with considerable asperity. 'All right, Barty, but there'll be no second chance. None. I'm acting against my better judgment.'

Fraser crossed the room but couldn't think precisely what to say. 'Sorry,' was all he could manage.

Giles brightened. 'OK. Forget it. But, while you've been sweating out too much Armagnac, I've been busy and the news is far from good. My company delivered two dozen cases of wine to L'Esprit restaurant. The Chambertin came from that batch. They were delivered a week ago and only one bottle besides the Chambertin had been tried. There had been no complaints about that but, having tasted the remainder, we agree that all the Corton, Volnay and the Clos Vougeot taste exactly the same as the duff Chambertin.'

'Well, one thought I've had,' opined Fraser 'is that the restaurateur must be ruled out. His clientele know their wines far too well for him to get away with a fraud as blatant as this. We've got to go one step backwards to your delivery man, then to your cellars and then back to Beaune.'

'If the problem's with the merchants in Beaune, then that's equally ruinous. If the integrity of the négociants is doubted, then the value of our stocks will be slashed. Sales will plummet and, moments later, one receives an embarrassing telephone call from the Bank.'

'Liabilities plenty, assets nil,' said Frank. 'I see what you mean.'

'What about the bottles? Was this a label switch, or was this the original bottle with different wine put in?'

'There's not a clue. You know as well as I do that almost no wine comes in numbered bottles and one green bottle looks the same as the next. It doesn't *look* as though the labels have been tampered with. A fairly professional job, I'd say.'

'You'd better check other deliveries made that day . . . by all your drivers. Meantime, I'm coming down to your premises this afternoon to get working.'

'That's more like it. No time to lose.' The two men drew close together and, as their eyes met, the old grip of fellowship clamped them together, tighter than a hug, more meaningful than a kiss.


NEW YORK

Smoky Levante was a typical New Yorker. Home had been a slum on West 152nd Street, where his one ambition had been to get away, to hit the big time, and there weren't many ways to hit the big time when you was just a no-good black boy from a family of ten. Especially with your Maw dead for fifteen of the twenty years of your life, and your father spending his days bouncing balls on street corners, his nights in Central Park mugging the unwary.

Had he been a foot taller, Smoky might have made it big in basketball but, at five feet ten inches, he was no different from the other guys on the block, except for an extra dash of daring and disregard for human life. He'd started with larceny from tourist hotels, before graduating to armed robbery. Then one day it had happened: a stranger had knocked on his door and hired him. He'd got his first job as a hit man. Since then business had been profitable. Eight bullets—eight deaths.

It was 10.15 p.m. in New York, 3.15 a.m. in London, as Smoky turned off neon-lit Times Square and headed for the Hudson River, down West 43rd. Darkness never falls on Times Square, which is just as well because it's dangerous anyway, full of junkies, muggers and dope-peddlers. As he moved cross-town the streets darkened, the sidewalks became less busy, the number of white faces more rare. In the shadows stood the occasional figure, maybe lighting a reefer, maybe clutching a knife, maybe trying a knee-trembler with a two-buck whore of indeterminate sex.

A trilby tipped over the embittered young features, his shoulders broad, hand on his gun, Smoky felt comfortable, impregnable. He had a job to do, no sweat. Kill Hubert Zeeler. No sweat. For why? He knew not and cared less. It paid well and it was better than work.

The shadowy silhouette of West Side Highway appeared in front of him and, from above, came the endless chain of lights, piercing the darkness. In the distance the wail of a police siren rose and fell somewhere along 10th Avenue as Smoky turned into 11th and then melted into the doorway of a time-blackened building. The lower floors were storerooms, with offices above, but everyone had long since gone home. As quickly as his movement stopped he was invisible, black as the atmosphere, as deep in its menace. He thought back to the photograph which he'd been given, which he had memorized and destroyed. Confident that he'd make no mistake, he settled in to wait. He had ten minutes in hand.

# LONDON

Full of good food and wine from an evening at the Garrick Club, Fraser hadn't noticed the chill easterly wind until he got home where a blast of warm air greeted him. He opened the door and looked with pleasure at the surroundings, now that he had discarded all the modern nonsense of Stage House. The expense had been absurd but furnishing the place with interesting pieces from Bond Street, Kensington Church Street and Sloane Avenue had been a pleasure. Every chair seemed to stretch out an invitation to be relaxed in, urging the chance to wallow in the depths of its comfort. The golden thickness of the pile carpet, the skilled blending of colours on the walls and imaginative use of lighting, gave the sitting-room a sense of timelessness and relaxation which struck Fraser on every return.

As he dialled Giles le Breton's home number and waited for an answer, he glanced around the room, making mental notes of other items which would enhance the room, a good French carriage clock and perhaps an Impressionist painting topping the list.

'Giles! I've been working overtime, making up for this morning.'

'Good God! What have you been doing?'

'I've been at the Garrick. Been studying those invoices and delivery notes which you gave me this afternoon. All the wine which went to L'Esprit was delivered by your chap Bragshaw. He did other deliveries that day but that particular load was a one off. Is that unusual?'

'No. But Bragshaw?' Giles thought for a moment. 'I doubt he's got the brains. What you're talking about is one man opening a wooden case or carton of wine and switching the contents.'

'I'll check him out. Been with you long?'

'Several years. Never been in any trouble either, as far as I can recall. Anyway, changing the subject, I've implemented a system whereby random samples are taken from loads awaiting delivery.'

'Did you check out whether any of your colleagues have had any trouble?'

'No. Not yet. Someone might start linking the change of menu at L'Esprit the other night with my questions. I'll just have to leave it for the moment. But no one's volunteered anything.'

'I wrote to David Bream. Told him that my expulsion was illegal and that I was going to act for you and for whomsoever I wanted, to mitigate my loss.'

'Is that right in law?'

'Probably. Difficult to prove but I expect that David Bream dragooned the rest of them into agreeing with him to dismiss me. If I could show that, then the expulsion must be invalid because they can't expel me without a hearing. If, on the other hand, they were all agreed to expel me without any canvassing, they're entitled to reach a decision without telling me.'

'And if they were to say that you were ever . . . drunk in the office?'

'Never. I fell asleep once after lunch but that was following the precedent of our greatest judges.'

'I'm glad you've taken the battle to them!'

# NEW YORK

Far from the smooth, taken-for-granted elegance of Belgravia, Smoky Levante was standing alone in the inky blackness of the doorway to the offices and warehouse on 11th Avenue. The stench of maturing trash hung heavily in the humidity of the night air. It seemed to rise from the sidewalk, fall from the buildings, penetrate the clothing, soak the skin and pollute the souls of the citizens of New York, yet Smoky never noticed it, for his life had always been full of filth, smells and corruption.

He looked at his watch. Hubert Zeeler was late. Surprising that, seeing as he was collecting his dough for the visits to New Orleans and Seattle. But Smoky had all the time in the world, nothing better to do, nothing he'd rather be doing than waiting for an unsuspecting prey. The sallow face, the wispy blackness of his beard gave warning of the menace which was the man, but after dark there was no warning, just an anonymous blackness capable of dispensing life and death with ungodly power.

The lights of a slowly moving cab caught his attention. Smoky's instructions had been plain. Let Zeeler quit the cab, pay off the driver, and then shoot him. Dress it up as any other mugging, just another statistic for the overworked computers at Police Headquarters.

The cab stopped just across the sidewalk from him, its headlights pinpointing some steam rising from a subway grid. As the man got out, Smoky could see him plainly. It was Zeeler, fresh back from Seattle, eager to collect his money, eager to cut and run.

'Wait here, willya,' the man told the driver.

Smoky was surprised, for Zeeler had been told to meet

his contact in a first-floor office. But what the hell! Play it by ear. See what happens.

Zeeler looked around him, checking his bearings and, on seeing the door he wanted, walked towards it with no sign of fear on his face as he stepped into the shadows. His right hand was firmly in his jacket pocket, a real giveaway that he was armed, but to no avail for it never left his pocket. Smoky's shot hit him from four yards, bursting into Zeeler's chest. Death was instantaneous as the supply of blood to the brain was diverted into an immediate, gushing stain on the front of the denim jacket.

No sooner had the body fallen than Smoky rifled the pockets, taking wallet and credit card folder. It was the work of seconds for a man of his experience and he did it while keeping half an eye across the sidewalk, gun aimed at the cab-driver, who was still wondering what to do. Fifteen years of driving in New York had taught him a great deal. Intervention was a pastime for the dead. As the shot had rung out, his instinct had been to duck and then, as he dared to peer across the sidewalk, he saw the crouching figure of a black man.

He was about to start the engine and get as much burnt tyre as possible between himself and the mugger, when the figure on the sidewalk advanced towards him, gun in hand. His intention was obvious and the approach was too quick for him to get away. The bullet hit him just as the engine roared into life. The single shot was again enough, smashing the man's Greek features, exploding deep in his brain. Well pleased, Smoky flung open the door, threw out the dead man, jumped in himself and crashed the automatic into 'Drive'. With a screech of tyres, he accelerated rapidly, hitting the lights at the end of the block at sixty, taking a left, a couple of rights and then another left. Satisfied that there were no pursuers, he abandoned the car and ran in the direction of the subway. Mission accomplished. Successfully too. Smoky

Levante don't make no mistakes. No, sir! They don't come no cleverer than Smoky. He sure was pleased as he approached the entrance to the subway. On looking down, he saw the patches of blood from his victim staining his clothes. Not so good. No subway. Best walk.

After Smoky had disappeared from the abandoned cab, it stood in silence attracting no attention from anyone. But then, from within, came a suspicion of movement as Annie Maguire squeezed her tiny figure from off the floor of the back seat, where she had slumped after the first shot had been fired. In her black trouser suit, she had lain there, unseen, during the brief, terrifying drive. The heavy grille separating driver from passengers obscured her presence from Smoky, clever Smoky, who had never suspected that she was there. But Annie had seen him, just for a second, as he sped down the block and it was a face she would remember for ever.

In the distance she could hear the wail of sirens playing a lament for her dead lover. But she had seen the killer and she would never forget him.

## LONDON

There was a rare intensity to the blue of the sky as Bartholomew Fraser walked down the wide expanse of Constitution Hill. At 7.00 a.m. the traffic was still light, the occasional taxi able to speed to its destination unhindered. For a rare moment, Fraser was reminded of the Provençal sky, such was the depth of colour which the morning sunlight contributed to the solid brick wall of the Palace grounds.

It was a pleasing walk and, with every pace, he could believe that the muscles in his leg were getting stronger, that the likelihood of his knee giving way was less real. He noticed with satisfaction that he was able to breathe in for ten paces, breathe out for ten. Not as good as at Oxford but a big improvement on even a month before and he still had another stone to lose.

There was a smile of satisfaction as he turned into Jermyn Street, where he barely noticed the Wren church as he gazed at the purveyors of fine cheeses, fine wines and outstanding shoes for the gentry.

Inside the Health Centre he was met by the resident trainer. ' 'Morning, Mr Fraser,' said Grunt Gordon, so called because he encouraged the clientele to make as much noise as they wanted while suffering the rigours of his circuit training.

' 'Morning, Grunt.'

'You've got five minutes to change.'

Stripped and ready for action, Fraser was no longer conscious of the scars which ploughed a white furrow down his thigh and criss-crossed his kneecap. Even his limp seemed less important, as he struggled into a routine of press-ups, back contractors and burpees. Into the swimming pool for twenty lengths breast-stoke. Then on his back. And all the while during the routine, sometimes consciously, sometimes unconsciously, his mind was thinking of the previous day and the arrangements for the day ahead. This morning he would be chatting to the van driver, having eliminated the cellar man the previous day. It hadn't been difficult, but then objectivity provides insight . . . and experience had bred confidence in his own judgment. One visit to the cellars had satisfied him that the cellar man could be eliminated.

'Mr Fraser!' The solicitor's thoughts were interrupted by Grunt Gordon. 'I've seen a pregnant woman swim quicker than that. You're daydreaming.' The moustached face was bent low over the pool. 'Twenty more lengths, then. Non-stop.'

Fraser stood in the shallow end, eyes dimmed by

exhaustion. 'You realize I come here . . . to enjoy myself.'

Grunt Gordon had heard it all before. 'Twenty lengths, I said.' He turned his attention to another client as Fraser set off once again on the lapping. Now, what had he been thinking? Ah! That's right, the cellar man. Oh, to be down there now, with that smell of history oozing from the arched, blackened brickwork, its temperature cool and constant, as it guarded line upon line, rack upon rack of priceless wines of every vintage since the nineteenth-century. Mixed with the musty subterranean smell came the aroma of sawdust, of alcohol, of barrels of brandy maturing in long lines.

Of course Digby Sugden, the cellar man, had known nothing of the reasons for the visit. He'd known Fraser for many years, both as customer and friend, so that the solicitor's arrival had been no surprise when the pretext was to discuss the merits of the 1980 vintage.

'Just one of that case,' Fraser had began, 'and put me down for three cases of the Chablis, although it sounds as if I'd be better off buying some of the proven years for my reds.'

'I would if I were you, sir.' The cellar man was always respectful. 'Some of our 1970's are still good value.'

Fraser smiled but his thoughts were of the Chambertin at L'Esprit. 'I'd like to think so. What about 1969? Have you anything really good from that year?'

'The Aloxe Corton. Or you might prefer the Nuits St Georges Pruliers.'

'Maybe.' Fraser was thoughtful for a moment. 'What about some Chambertin.'

'We have none. The original stocks have all been sold, although we bought in a couple of cases not so long ago. It was all we could get and even that was difficult. But for our reputation with our négociants in Beaune, there would have been no chance.'

'And none of that left?'

'No. The restaurant trade took that. And who could blame them?' The cellar man had then taken Fraser back to his scruffy office, laden with old invoices and dirty glasses. 'Of course, we could buy in some Chambertin from other sources.' The words were said disparagingly, with the man's gloomy face looking more hang-dog than ever. 'But le Breton and Co. would never do that. Our reputation is far too important.'

'I know. Anyway, put me down for three cases of the Volnay 1969, would you?' Fraser was perched on the edge of the man's desk and was idly flicking through a copy of *Decanter* magazine. 'Do I hear you're retiring soon?'

'I'm afraid so. Yes. Forty-nine years service, interrupted only by the War.'

'Not much fun retiring, with all this inflation.' Fraser was fishing.

'No. But we've been prudent. Maisie and I paid off our mortgage when her Dad died. Our place is just on the Kent side of Lee Green. Not as bad as it sounds down there, neither.'

'I'm sure.' Fraser nodded politely, while privately thinking that he would take a lot of persuading to switch Belgravia for Lee Green. 'But income-wise? After all, that's the real problem with inflation. Assets are fine but you've still got to eat. Do the company have a pension scheme?'

'Yes, but not index-linked like those lucky blighters in Whitehall neither.' He paused. 'But then I'm not in a position of laying down the rules like they are.'

'It is something of an advantage, making your own rules, isn't it? We could all be better off, every man jack of us, if it lay in our power to recommend a scheme and then implement it as well. I should think the Civil Service Union saw Ted Heath coming. Fell for that, didn't he? Sounded so reasonable, all this index-linking at the time.

Now it's going to bankrupt the country within thirty years.'

'I shan't be around then.' Digby Sugden switched off the electric kettle. 'Anyway, the company are good to me. They've promised me a bonus, calculated on the five years' profits up to retirement.'

'That sounds useful. Make sure you invest it wisely. Is it to be Granny Bonds or Château Lafite?' Although Fraser's tone was jocular, he knew that the interview was over. Not even the greatest fool would destroy the company's profits when his bonus on retirement was calculated by reference to them. There was no sense in that.

'Well, sir, if you'll excuse me, I've got the bottles to turn.'

'I'm sorry, I expect I was holding you up. But it's always nice talking to you.'

As he lapped and turned, lapped and turned down the warm waters of the pool, locked in a world of spume and aching limbs, he had no doubts about Digby Sugden. He stopped and sat on the edge of the pool, his nerves still twitching uncontrollably and his breath coming painfully. Grunt Gordon arrived, looking indecently fit and unruffled in his immaculate white tracksuit and red running shoes.

'It's all right for you,' gasped Fraser. 'I've never seen you doing any of these exercises.'

'I don't need to. I can keep fit with sex four times a day.'

'Liar!' Fraser clasped Grunt's ankle and, with a quick push from his other hand, unbalanced the instructor, who landed in the water with an undignified splash. Waiting till the man surfaced again, Fraser added. 'That'll cool your ardour.'

'You're just jealous, that's all. I'll still be pulling birds when I'm twice your age.'

'You're twice my age already.'

★

The telephone was ringing upstairs as he turned the house key. Fatigued by too much swimming, he was unable to hurry but the caller was persistent or patient and was still there when Fraser picked up the receiver.

'Bartholomew Fraser speaking.'

The voice at the other end was female. 'Ah! Mr Fraser. My name is Emma Fry-Cripps. I don't think you know me?'

'No, I don't believe I do,' but even as he said it, Fraser was rather wishing that perhaps he did. It was *that* kind of voice.

'I'm a researcher with the *Daily Topic*.' Fraser knew the *Daily Topic*. It was a Fleet Street tabloid with increasing circulation, although the standard of its news content was level with that of the *Beano*. For tit and bum journalism it was superb. London clubs had it but always in leather-bound folders.

'What do you research, Miss Fry-Cripps?'

'I'm the Topical Topic column. Personal assistant to Sheridan Bullough.' Fraser recognized the name of one of Fleet Street's party creeps, the name of a hack with a nose for the prurient. His groan was not inward and was intended for Miss Fry-Cripps to hear.

'And how can I help Mr Sheridan Bullough?' The solicitor recalled the nudge-nudge journalism of the column when it had covered the death of his wife. The accident had been news, for his wife had been well known in Society circles, having been Deb of the Year in the mid-Sixties. The whole concept of the column was nauseating, yet its innuendo held sway in the land, its daily euphemisms bringing peepshow porn to the people.

'I understand that a Writ has been issued against you by your former firm. We'd like a bit of background.'

'And you're one of Sheridan Bullough's leg women, are you?'

The caller laughed, appreciating the double entendre. 'You could say that.' Bullough's penchant for legs was well known far beyond Fleet Street.

'Yes. There is a Writ against me. End of story.'

'Not so. Not quite, anyway. Would you care to comment?'

'No.'

'Why not?'

'Sub judice. Surely even the *Daily Topic* knows that?' Fraser's voice was firm without being angry.

'But I want your point of view.' Emma was used to getting her own way.

'And if I don't give it?'

'We'll write the story anyway. Our way. Without your point of view.' She let it sink in for a moment, before adding an unnecessary threat. 'And you don't want that, do you?'

Bartholomew Fraser had seen the column often enough to know that she was right. 'You win. You want some background?'

'That's right. I knew you'd see reason.'

'OK. I'll give you some non-attributable quotes.'

'Over the phone won't do. I want to meet you.'

'Then you'd better come over here. I'm in Belgravia Mews.'

'No. I never visit the homes of strange men. Not before bedtime.'

Fraser heard the words and was surprised at the confidence of the voice, which placed the speaker as being in her twenties. 'All right. Meet me at the Wig and Pen Club in Fleet Street?'

'The Wig and Pen! I wouldn't be seen dead in there. Full of lawyers and journalists. And don't suggest El Vino's either. Meet me in Sancho's Wine Bar in Chancery Lane at twelve. Don't be late. It's fine if you beat the rush.'

Bartholomew Fraser arrived sharp at twelve noon, with just a shade of trepidation. He'd been undecided as to what to wear when meeting a gossip columnist. Should it be the pin-striped solicitor, or should he be off duty in casual clothing? He decided to compromise with a grey suit, wine-coloured shirt and tie.

Inside Sancho's it was gloomy until his eyes became accustomed to the light. The place was heavy with green drapes, sawdust and endless bottles of cheap undrinkable wine, which nevertheless was cheerfully drunk every lunch-time with rare beef sandwiches and a veneer of unwarranted sophistication. The room was nearly empty.

'Has Miss Fry-Cripps arrived?' he enquired of the barman.

'No. But she ordered that corner table over there. You'll have a drink?'

'Orange juice, please. Plenty of ice.'

'OK. But she ordered champagne and a couple of glasses. They're already there.'

'Did she, by Jove! I'll have the orange juice anyway.'

Fraser sat down and, having studied the snack menu four times over with increasing uninterest, realized that she was now half an hour late, despite her entreaty to him to be punctual. It gave him time to think about his interview with the van driver, Arthur Henry Bragshaw. It had been difficult to know what to make of him. The man had been straightforward, had answered questions with confidence but uncertainty. He could recall no particular delivery any more than another. Life was full of deliveries, wasn't it. 'I mean, one day's the same as the next, isn't it, guv'nor. I mean, I'm always delivering to L'Esprit, Claridge's, Boulestin's and that. Just one long line of bleedin' traffic jams and lugging cases of wine about. But it's better than the dole queue, ain't it, mate?'

Of course Bragshaw had asked why he was being questioned but Fraser had been as evasive in his

generality as had Bragshaw. The enquiry agent's report
had revealed nothing but Bragshaw had to be a suspect
until eliminated. He'd remain a long shot, though. She
was three-quarters of an hour late and arrived just as he
was practising various lines of indignation.

Emma was disarming. Her voice had told no lies, for
she was indeed twenty-two years old, with long fair hair,
which hung luxuriant round her small face, like a judge's
wig. The eyes were big and dancing, the mouth small and
playful. But it wasn't just the face which captivated and
neither was it the figure which, while neat, was nothing
exceptional. It was the *presence* which she generated.
The room was instantly full of her, despite the fact that
she stood only five feet five inches. She exuded confidence
from the casual swing of her shoulder-bag to the breezy
greeting, with no hint of an apology or an excuse for
lateness.

'But aren't you just dishy?' she exclaimed loud enough
for heads to turn from all directions. Fraser, rising to his
feet, faltered, sensing that he was attracting unnecessary
attention. The rehearsed lines of indignation were
forgotten.

'Nice to meet you, Miss Fry-Cripps.' He managed to get
it out with difficulty, feeling that his speech was being
listened to by half the secretaries and lawyers of Chancery
Lane. Nevertheless, he managed a generous smile, as he
flourished an arm towards the empty chair, his voice
sounding deep and throaty.

'Call me Emma. And I shall call you Barty. That's what
you were called at school, wasn't it?' She flung herself into
the chair and flicked her hair into position.

'You're remarkably well informed.'

'And you're remarkably ill-mannered for not opening
that champagne.' The eyelashes fluttered. 'I thought I
was meeting a gentleman.' She picked up his empty glass
of orange, sniffing it suspiciously. 'Ugh! Orange juice.

There'll be no more of that round here.'

'I happen to like it.' Fraser was defensive, struck by the blitzkrieg of her arrival. It sounded stuffy and so he grasped the bottle of icy champagne, condensation running down its green sides. He was breaking all his new rules but the sight of it and the tension of her presence made his tongue feel parched, his liver deprived.

'I always drink champagne. Any time. Lunch-time, dinner-time, at parties, in bed—before and after. Even during, sometimes. You know, it really is the *only* drink.'

'For the drinking classes.'

'You're not drinking?'

'Yes. I might have a little. But I don't normally at lunch-time.'

'Why?'

'Too early in the day.'

'Drying out?' The deep green eyes gazed at him, as her elegant, slim fingers flipped open a packet of King Size. He found himself captivated by each of her movements, by the red and black face of the watch on the slender brownness of her arm, by the giant size of the unusual stone in the ring on her finger, by the red trouser suit, which had been tailor-made for a dwarf. On her it left six inches of bare Marbella-browned midriff, invitingly visible.

'Me? Drying out? Just wiser, that's all.' It was partly true. Somehow, he couldn't admit the complete truth to her, especially not knowing the ground rules of what was going to be on the record and what was going to be left unpublished.

She blew smoke at him. 'Don't believe you.'

In his uncertainty Fraser said nothing. She'd probably spent the last two hours digging up the dirt. 'Cheers.' 1973 Taittinger. It was crisp, delicious and made better by the company.

'So you really are human.' Her voice conveyed surprise.

'But where are the worst scars? In your mind? Or on your leg? No one seems to have seen your leg since the accident.' She leant across so that, for a second, her long hair brushed his cheek and she clamped her hand on his thigh. 'It's not wooden, is it?'

'No.' he was momentarily lost for words.

'You'd look better without that stuffy old legal suit.'

'And you,' Fraser retorted, 'should have bought that outfit in the right size.' He put on his paternal solicitor role, voice deepening and face solemn. 'My dear: you should spend less on champagne. In that get-up you'll catch a chill.' Even as he was speaking Fraser was wondering what had come over him. He hadn't felt so frivolous for years. Was it Emma? Was it the champagne? Certainly her attitudes were infectious.

Emma's look was quizzical and she decided to regain the initiative by changing the subject. In her gossip column world she was unused to meeting people with brains, more used to the crowd with hyena laughs and no grey matter where it mattered.

'Your wife was quite a hit on the social scene, wasn't she? I've read a few cuttings.'

'Yes.'

'And the accident was your fault?'

'You've done your homework.'

'And it's hit you hard.'

'Well done! Yes, I've been ill.' His voice betrayed his bitterness but then he recovered, pushing out of his mind the vision of the bend in the road and the slithering feeling of lost control. 'It's healing. All I need is time.'

The waiter's arrival with salmon mousse cut short her comment. 'I trust it's not like the *rubbish* you provided last week, George. *That* was more like rock salmon.'

'I do assure you it's delicious, delightful.'

'We'll be the judge of that—but thank you, George. That will be all.' There had been no malice in her voice and the richness of her smile blunted the barb. Nevertheless Fraser, trained in the discreet, well-ordered legal profession, felt uncomfortable, taken aback.

'So her death hit you hard?' she resumed. 'And you never remarried?'

'No.'

'Why not?'

As if it were the most interesting thing in the world, Fraser studied his cuff-link and then the patterns in the sawdust on the floor, before answering. 'It's too soon. It would hurt . . . too much.' He looked up to see the reaction. 'Oh look! We're not here to talk about this. Let's get on with the interview, shall we?'

'But you've never been seen flirting around?'

'Not in your circles anyway. I don't go in for that sort of thing.'

'Not turned gay, have you? That would make a good story.'

'Publish what you like. Call me "Fay the Gay" if you want to. No one whose opinion I value reads your column anyway. But let's just stick to what you really want to know. Or is that it?'

She poured more champagne. 'Sorry. It's just my style. The human angle interests me, the human bent, you might say. OK, then. What about this writ? Will you fight it? It's to stop you acting for any of the clients of your old firm, isn't it?'

'Yes. And I'm going to fight it.'

'What's it all about?'

'My partners thought that they could use my office space to better advantage. You see, I'd been away a great deal since the accident. Hospitals, clinics, nursing homes. Everywhere. But they're terrified I'm going to pinch their clients.'

'And would you?'

'As their idea of work is downing pink gins and listening

to the boring reminiscences of a former naval officer, then my answer is yes.' She smiled and scribbled down a note. 'That's off the record of course. But you wanted the truth.'

'Can you defend the action?'

'Yes. And I can counterclaim too.'

'Can I quote you on that?'

'Yes. But I'd prefer if you didn't do it directly. Sub judice and all that. I'm sure you don't want to be done for Contempt of Court. You could publish something like "sources close to Bartholomew Fraser indicate that he intends to react sharply to the application for an Injunction and will also counterclaim. Friends say that he is retaining Hobart's, the well-known litigation lawyers in the City. Mr Fraser personally declined to comment, on the grounds that it was sub judice." ' Fraser pushed his plate to one side. 'Is that OK?' He could see the glazed look on her face.

'Splendid! Just what we need to boost circulation! Our competitors will be terrified! I'll have to work on it a bit. Beef it up. Something on the lines of man-about-town Bart Fraser, well known wine buff, now spends his days in his chic mews cottage rather than the daily grind of life in the solicitors' offices in which he was a partner." That's the sort of thing I've got in mind. I say! What about a photograph? I see you as the British Bulldog type. Kenneth More on the Bridge.'

'With a bone between my teeth? Or perhaps wearing my Hello Sailor T-shirt?'

'You're very photogenic, you know. If you don't find something suitable, then we'll print something unsuitable.'

'I'll lend you the X-ray photograph of my hip joint. You could use that if you like. Your editor could use it for "Spot the Break"—a variation on "Spot the Ball".'

'Now, now, Barty!' She wagged a slender finger at him.

'Solicitors don't crack jokes. That won't do at all.' She grasped his leg again. 'Go on—please dig out a photo.'

'OK. I'm sure I've got one somewhere, doing my Marty Feldman impression.' They were interrupted by the Brie.

Emma pressed it with her knife. 'Deliciously soft. Just right. But George, do bring the port. There's a dear.'

George pouted provocatively. 'It's coming.'

'So is the Resurrection. But do be a dear and hurry it all along.' She stubbed out her third cigarette and set about the cheese.

'Do you like this job? Prying and spying?'

She shrugged her shoulders, an exercise which revealed an extra two inches of midriff.

'Yes. It's a fun thing. I can't think of anything I wouldn't publish if I wanted to. You see, I'm giving the public what they want. Much better than the Common Agricultural Policy or the collapsing sales in the herring industry. Incest at Instow, bribery in Brighton, fornication in Fulham is what sells newspapers. Don't blame me—blame the public.'

By the time the champagne was finished, the Brie consumed and the port enjoyed, Fraser felt a mellowness come over him. 'It's been interesting talking to you, although sparring might have been a more appropriate word.'

She raised her eyes and looked at him hard. 'You think so?'

'So what about some dinner?'

'Tonight's out. It's the Archie Gallaher Memorial Ball at Quag's. *Everyone* will be there.'

'Except me.'

'And who are you?'

'Sufficiently important for you to be publishing tittle-tattle about me.'

'OK. Nearly everyone will be there.'

'Except me.'

'Except you. But tomorrow night's fine.'

'OK. But I might be in France by then.'

'Oh? Business?'

'Sort of. I'd rather not talk about it.' As a remark it was designed to make any gossip columnist alert and Emma Fry-Cripps was no exception. Her eyes glinted but she made no specific comment.

'I'll check out my diary. We could have fun if we're both free. If you're not in France.'

Fraser was about to reply when she rose, kissed him on the cheek and, with a swivel of hips, was gone, leaving the room feeling empty and himself feeling breathless, as if he'd been pirouetted by a tornado. For a few moments he sat staring without seeing. 'Quite a girl, isn't she?' It was George clearing the table.

Fraser jumped. 'Oh . . . oh yes!'

'She told me to leave you the bill.' For a moment Fraser's face dropped in surprise and then he found himself laughing, laughing loud and hard. Emma Fry-Cripps had the cheek of the devil.

By a quarter past five the same afternoon Fraser was back in Belgravia Mews, having sorted out the defence of the Injunction with his solicitors at their Dowgate Hill office. His affidavit sworn, his instructions plain and straightforward, there was nothing further which Fraser could do for the time being. He had barely added the water to the Earl Grey tea when Giles le Breton arrived.

'You're looking much better today, Barty.'

'Thanks. Always nice to hear that sort of thing. But it looks as though the burden of all this is hanging pretty heavily on you.'

Le Breton put down his red leather document case and tightly rolled umbrella. 'Not sleeping so well these days. I keep turning over all the facts. My company's in for a hiding.'

'Ridiculous!'

'Thank God I've got you to confide in, to talk to.' Giles accepted the aromatic tea and helped himself to a chocolate biscuit. 'There's no one else I can turn to, not about this sort of thing. Anyway, I can forget Bragshaw, can I?' His normally languid face looked furrowed and pallor replaced the polished pink look of days gone by. Le Breton wanted reassurance, positive answers, anything to pigeonhole the confusion of thoughts which were so troubling.

'I've got a Private Eye on him still—but so far nothing.'

'I suppose that's good news.'

'My guess is your problem's in France. If it were your staff, a random check would have found plenty of bogus wine. Are you sure no other shippers have been duped?'

'I dare not ask.'

'Well, just suppose they had. Would you have heard of it then?'

'No. I'm sure their reaction would be the same as mine. Better to burn one's backside on the mouth of the volcano than permit an eruption of red hot gossip.'

'I'm going to Beaune as Bartholomew Fraser, Master of Wine—not as Bartholomew Fraser, solicitor. I've got one or two useful contacts, and if there's anything afoot, then I'd be amazed if they didn't know. I shall probably go the day after tomorrow.' As he spoke, his mind was on Emma, knowing that the only reason for putting back his departure was the hope of dinner with her the next evening.

'But what about your own case with Bream and Bream? Isn't that due to be heard on Friday?'

'It'll go ahead. I don't have to be there. I expect my solicitors will agree terms for an adjournment, in return for certain undertakings and arrangements to be made for a speedy trial.'

'Speedy trial? What's that?'

'A concept occasionally known to the Law.'

'Just so long as it doesn't interfere with what you're doing for me. You're far too important.'

'Dinner tonight?'

'Thanks, but no. I'm saying goodbye to . . . a friend.'

'Anyone I know?'

The reply was hurried. 'No. No, I doubt it.'

Fraser noticed the slight unease and didn't pursue the matter any further. 'Have a good time anyway.'

'Thanks. By the way, Barty, do you regard me as a suspect?'

'Until I can positively eliminate you—yes, I do.'

'Thank you. Thank you very bloody much.'

'Well, you asked. But I don't think it's likely. I can't see what your motive would be at the moment.'


## SAVANNAH, GEORGIA

It was approaching midday and the temperature was still rising. A hot, damp towel of humidity was clamped over the predominantly black residents of the city. Everyone was talking about the need for thunder and a mighty storm to clear the air. The flowers in Wright Square and Forsyth Park needed to be revitalized if they were to give pleasure before dying. In the hot stillness, there came from the Savannah River the occasional hooted blast of a cargo vessel as it passed the statue of Florence Martus, just as ships had done when she had stood at this spot in her lifetime, waving and watching for the return of her loved one. It had been fifty years since she had died but the statue ensured that the tradition would live for ever.

Savannah, colonial capital of the state of Georgia, thriving port on the Atlantic seaboard, had survived a chequered history since its foundation in 1733 by James

Oglethorpe and a few settlers. The city had grown up, been raped by fire and raped again and yet had somehow survived, until today, on this hot summer morning, the old houses of the original settlers and the new office blocks were blended together in relative comfort.

The man from New York descended the iron-balustraded stairway to Factor's Walk and then strolled along Riverfront Park, before sitting down beside a small fountain. Upstream was the giant bridge, thronged with vehicles, and further up in the distance were the many quays and warehouses of the docks. Joe Mocari, wine merchant, looked at his watch. If Nat Coburn hadn't missed his connection at Atlanta, then he should just be landing at Savannah Airport now, after the long flight from San Francisco.

They didn't meet often, Nat Coburn from California and Joe Mocari from New York, but then there had been no need. Things had been going too well.

It was a bad day to be fat, indeed the Savannah climate never treated the overweight too kindly. It was, therefore, with an effort that he stood up and made his way, heavily dripping, towards the entrance of the Hyatt Regency Hotel, which now dominated the waterfront. In the giant atrium of the hotel it was cool and the beads of perspiration stopped dripping from Mocari's forehead. A small band played mellow music and three glass-fronted lifts glided silently up and down, ever watchful on events below. No one and nothing seemed hurried, but then that was typical of the Deep South, with its lazy, drawling speech and the rolling, slouching gait of the inhabitants. Savannah was a city of relaxation, of taking it easy, and some did that just too literally. The wine merchant from New York was scarcely the only criminal in Savannah that day.

As the temperature rose outside to 92 degrees, Nat Coburn was relieved to exchange the cramped cab for the air-conditioned atrium. Aged thirty-four, he'd learnt about life in some advanced schools of dereliction. His lean, six-foot body showed no sign of wear and tear and his face was a mask, unsullied by the problems and crises which he had faced and survived.

He knew that the pace would tell eventually. Indeed, if he kept on at the same pace, it was bound to show soon. You couldn't rise every morning before dawn to check the vines, supervise the winery, keep tabs on the finance, keep the punters happy, without jeopardizing the fuse. But Nat Coburn had no intention of going on too long. He'd bought a plot for a villa in the Virgin Islands and soon he'd be there, rich and carefree. A manager could run Minstrel Creek winery for him. By the end of the year he'd know for sure, but conservatively he was reckoning on increasing his assets by two or maybe three million. Better still, he'd get those lousy shareholders off his back.

Experience had taught him to travel light, to make light of travel, and as he stood in the atrium, gazing at the hotel rising all round him, those looking at him saw a man without any sign of the long flight, a man with a pale blue, lightweight suit still crease-free, eyes alert and without the slightest hint of perspiration around the temples. Coburn's brown hair was cut very short and parted with precision on the left side; the features were regular and bronzed by the everyday Californian sun. Girl-friends had come easily but then so had their departures. The narrowing eyes and the meanness of the lips should have given a warning that nothing, but nothing, would prevent Coburn's rush for success. To him, even the golden-brown bodies, whether lying naked by his pool or in a remote motel room, were just ego-fuel rather than something to be savoured for an end in itself.

Nat Coburn was a respecter of no one, not even Joe Mocari, fat, overweight Joe Mocari, whose forty-seven years in New York City had given him an instinct for survival.

'Hi, Nat,' said Mocari.

'Joe! Good to see you. Flight OK?'

'I'm here, so I guess it was.' The laconic style was typical of the man.

'Fine! Fine!' Mocari's voice, in keeping with his face, had all the pugnacious greasiness of a childhood on West 10th Street, near 6th Avenue in Downtown Manhattan. He was a third-generation Italian/American, flabby-jowled, heavy with years of pasta and miles of spaghetti. For a man of forty-seven he looked ten years older, nearly bald, forehead creased by the stress of keeping ahead of the game New York style. It hadn't been easy. In "Little Italy" he knew that it paid to have "friends" but Joe had preferred to be alone, building up his own wine import business, shunning the Mob, while never showing disrespect. An uneasy laissez-faire relationship existed but Joe could never forget that the Mafia had tentacles round the neck of much of the wine business, both in France and New York City. Directly or indirectly, wines and spirits were part of their legitimate business and Joe knew better than to step outside the bounds which had been beaten out between them. But they weren't the only big league criminals in the American liquor trade. Mocari understood this well.

Joe felt safe in meeting Coburn in the backwater of sleepy old Savannah, for here he was anonymous, a feeling unknown in New York, where every sidewalk seemed to tell tales. Among the teeming millions in Manhattan, Mocari felt constantly observed, known, possessed, just as if the city were a small place, a hamlet in which people knew the girl you were dating, the girl you were two-timing, the people with whom you did business, the state of your bank balance and the softer points for future blackmail and extortion.

'Eaten yet?' enquired Coburn.

'No. I was reckoning on eating well tonight. For now I'd rather drop by the coffee shop, pick up a burger and get into the hard talking.'

'All-rightee,' Coburn mimicked the locals. 'You-all have a good day and a Big Mac gumbo-style?' Both men laughed. 'Anyway, it's good to see you, Joe. We've a thing or two to talk about. So just give me ten minutes and I'll see you at the bar.'

Later, when they had eaten, they left the hotel and stood by the throng of traffic on Bay Street. Still not a word had been said about the business in hand but Coburn, even more than Mocari, was paranoid about confidentiality.

The blue skies of noon had given way to the hot oppressiveness of three o'clock and the horizon was heavily tinged with grey haze. Thunder was an hour away as they waited to cross and walk up Bull Street to take a look at Wright Square, as recommended by the concierge. In the stickiness of the heat even Coburn felt clammy, despite his lightweight suit.

Wright Square was cool, heavily shaded and spoiled by the scattering of winos, snoozing the afternoon away under the heavy branches.

'Sure is a beautiful city.' Coburn glanced about him. 'Kinda reminds me of London — Lincoln's Inn Fields — or maybe it was Brighton. Regency buildings, wrought-ironwork and a sense of dignity. Ever been there?'

'Nope. But I ain't got no feelings about no place. A place is a place, period. So this is Savannah. There ain't no skyscrapers, ain't no London Bridge, ain't no Vatican nor no Eiffel Tower. So, who cares. There's beer, food and I guess there's some dames here to screw. Who cares about wrought-ironwork and all that crap.'

'I should have known better than to wax poetic with

you Joe. So let's get down to business. Tell me about New York.'

'Hubert Zeeler's dead. The only witness was a cab-driver and the guy I hired, Smoky Levante, shot him too. The cops think it was a mugging and no different from at least eight other deaths in the city that day.'

'Zeeler did a good job, particularly the fracas at Atkinson's in New Orleans. I saw the report. That was a good idea having a photographer there. Made a lot of news down there in Louisiana. Due to Zeeler's tour we've got little pockets throughout the US where people are thinking twice about French wines, just wondering if they're getting what they've paid for.'

Joe nodded his head. 'Trouble is, too many of our fellow countrymen won't admit that they know sweet fanny all about wines, can't tell Pepsi from champagne.'

'I've got Karen Schunberg in L.A. for the PR. When we're ready, she's gonna plait each of those threads into a rope and then loop it round the neck of the French wine industry.'

'And throttle it.' The wrinkles on Mocari's sweat-ridden forehead changed pattern as he grinned in anticipation. Perspiration trickled down the rivulets towards the squashed unpleasantness which was his nose.

'Karen's gonna hype this story into an international monster able to rear its head wherever she wants. It'll be front page in Paris and big news in London. All we need in Paris is someone to press the button. London's the same. I thought we might have had feedback by now but there's been nothing. Some real bum wine's gone to le Breton & Co. I'm pressing the button in London today.'

'You're some guy, Nat.' Mocari's admiration was real. 'You've got it all set up. There'll be rumours and innuendo everywhere. Those Frenchies are gonna take some pasting. But what about that shipment into Canada?'

'That story's gonna blow tomorrow. In rather less than twenty-four hours, Hermann Kressin will take a walk into the McMac Liquor Mart in downtown Dallas.'

'McMac!' Joe Mocari sounded concerned.

'Sure. There, he'll buy six bottles of their newly arrived Appellation Contrôlée Bourgogne Rouge. When he gets it home he'll taste it and file a complaint with McMac and with the US Customs, for the wine ain't Appellation Contrôlée Bourgogne Rouge at all. Suddenly McMac have got three million bottles of unsaleable wine and a lawsuit hanging over their heads. And we have coast to coast publicity.'

'You mean the McMac chain has bought the entire shipment?' There was panic on the listener's face.

'Sure. All three million bottles. They couldn't resist a bargain.'

'McMac!' breathed Mocari again. 'All three million! Jesus! Should I laugh or cry. Christ, they're gonna get their fingers so burnt. But hell, I wish I'd known that it was McMac you were setting up.' Mocari lit another cigarette. 'I mean, do you know who they are?' His voice sound incredulous.

'Sure I do. They're the biggest chain of Liquor Marts in the US. And Karen Schunberg's gonna have a field-day with them. She'll have examples at the top of the market from all round the US coupled now with the McMac rubbish at the bottom. You gotta believe that everyone's sure gonna be gunning for the French and Karen's gonna jog a few memories of the troubles in Bordeaux back along, point to the troubles in Germany, with the lorryloads of sugar being dumped in the wine. All that type of crap.'

Mocari was unimpressed. 'But hang on, Nat. I mean, do you really know who McMac are?'

'Like I said, the biggest liquor outlet.'

'But you know who's behind them?'

'Long-established corporation. HQ in Atlantic City, as I recall, they're headed up by some Senator.'

'Right. And his name's Greg Janus.'

'So what's new?'

'Only that Senator Janus is front man for a very unpleasant set-up. He's a pædophile and the gang found out, so they put him at the top for respectability. But it's Rudi Ramalpo and his hoods who pick up the cash from the bottom line.'

'Are they the Mob?'

'No. But about as rough. Especially if they've got three million bum bottles.'

For a moment there was silence, broken only by the occasional cough and splutter from a vagrant swigging at a bottle. When Coburn spoke it was quietly. 'Hell! You're well informed. That's all news to me. We're changing ball parks, aren't we?' It was not a question. It was a very obvious statement of fact. 'That's some type of problem! I should have checked it out with you when I knew McMac were the buyers but I never gave it a thought. I just saw the great publicity when the shit hit the fans. I sure don't wanna go round crossing big timers. No way, sir.'

'You're right there, Nat. There sure will be some shit flying around when McMac faces process and has three million bottles of unusable wine on its hands. And they ain't gonna take that lying down. They ain't gonna shrug no shoulders and put it down to experience. So OK, they'll get to make their lawyers claim on insurance, earn their dough, but you bet your last dime they're gonna be working on it and never stop until they find out the guys that screwed them. And they're dead. Believe me. Nat, you ain't mixing with Senator Janus—you're crossing one of the toughest families on the Eastern seaboard.'

'But it's too late to stop Hermann Kressin now. Whether we like it or not, McMac have got the wine.'

'But Kressin's the man's who's gonna blow that whistle.

Maybe nobody else will if he doesn't.'

'Joe—I sure respect your judgment but that whistle's gotta blow. There's too much money tied up. We gotta bring the French down now. You're forgetting how much it cost to set up that shipment. Don't forget, Joe, that wine's come from Italy, been imported into France, bottled and labelled in France as genuine French wine and then exported from Sète into Canada.'

'Well, I think you should call off this guy Kressin. Pay him off. Tell him the deal's off.'

'We're too far gone, Joe. We've gotta keep this thing moving. So McMac spells trouble. Unfortunate, but we've just gotta take that chance.'

'I don't like it.' Mocari was sullen now. 'I can see my name on a lousy bullet.'

Nat leant across and held Mocari's sleeve. 'Don't be dramatic, Joe! There ain't no way they're gonna trace us. Why should they? That's if you've been careful in New York.'

'Sure, I've been careful. No one can link me with Zeeler. No one can link me directly with the three million bottles. Hell, we've been careful enough in our dealings with the French.'

'That's more like it, Joe. We've been *professional*. We've gotta take that chance.'

'Well, I guess it's time you rang France, get your guy to expose some of the wine lying around in the Paris restaurants.'

'But what about the people who bottled the Italian wine in France?'

'Them? They don't know nothing. They don't even know the wine came from Italy. It was just a load of wine which they had to bottle and label. Our trouble's not in France—it's here.' Mocari's eyes were glazed. His shirt, bulging at every seam, was heaving with emotion as he lit yet another cigarette.

'Nat.' Mocari looked at Coburn, his eyes fearful. 'I've lived a lifetime in New York. I know how it works. Trouble in Times Square? I know about it before it happens. A Mob killing on the Upper East side? I can see it coming. New York?' His eyes closed for a moment as he considered his rhetorical question. 'I can smell shit or trouble there at a hundred yards.' Mocari stood up sharply. 'I just wish you'd call off Hermann Kressin.'

Coburn rose to follow him, his lean elegance contrasting with the squat fatness of his partner. 'No way, Joe.'

'Kinda nice attitude to your friend. Remind me to mention you in my will. You'll be inheriting real soon.'

'Quit it, Joe!' Coburn tried to put an arm on Joe's shoulder but Mocari shrugged it aside. 'You'll be able to lie low.'

'Lie low! Don't give me that crap. Ain't you just forgetting that we've still got the auction to get through? There's still work to be done about that. There ain't no way I can lie low.' Mocari watched for the 'Walk' sign to flash and then strode angrily across the road. At the other side he continued. 'Like, do I get the arrangements for the auction called off? Do I cancel all the arrangements for the wine being shifted to the docks at Bordeaux? Like, what do I tell the auctioneers here in Savannah? What do I say? Sorry, folks, it ain't coming. It ain't coming because I'm disappearing? Nat, we're too far down this particular shit-hole to get out.'

Coburn was worried. 'You New Yorkers are all the same. Ever dramatic, everything larger than life. You see the world in Technicolor, Cinerama, jumbo size. And things ain't that bad. No, of course we let the auction go ahead.'

'Well, just don't forget the flowers at the funeral. I want a big show, Nat.' Mocari wasn't joking. Angrily he left Coburn behind and made for the lift to the hotel's fifth floor.

The building shook to the first rumble of thunder. It was going to be some storm.


# LONDON

It was late afternoon and central London was unbearably hot. Large black clouds had swept up from the west. There was a stillness hanging over the City, compressing the noise of rush-hour traffic into an undispersed roar. The blast of horns gave away the irritation of the jam-packed drivers.

At least the noise failed to penetrate Belgravia Mews, but as Bartholomew Fraser peered out of the window he reckoned that someone, out Hounslow way was getting a downpour and that the Jumbos leaving Heathrow would find the first 5,000 feet somewhat choppy. His interest in the weather was more than casual, for he was booked on the morning crossing out of Folkestone and rough seas always brought out the worst in his stomach.

The telephone started to ring. 'Yes?'

'What did you think of my article, then?' It was Emma. 'Pretty bloody good, wasn't it?' She answered her own question before Fraser had a chance to say a word.

'If I hadn't liked it you'd have heard this morning, but where the hell did you find that old picture?'

'It was difficult. We had to go back a long way in our archives to find one which wouldn't *reduce* our readership. It was obviously taken at a very dark party.'

'It was.'

'But you can still see the bottle of claret under each eyeball.' Emma noticed the lengthy pause before the reply, a delay caused by Fraser's painful recollection of the night when the photograph had been taken and of his irritation at the damned photographer intruding on his privacy.

At last Fraser spoke. 'I'm sure you didn't phone to tell me how good you were at your job. Or to expect me to tell you the same thing. So what do you want?' He was surprised at the edge to his voice, sharpened by his recollection of that night of the photograph, that night in Chelsea, that night of the long moonlit drive back to Sussex, that night of strolling round the garden in the stillness of 3.00 a.m., before making love at length and with gentleness.

'You talked about dinner.'

'I thought you were busy.' It hadn't been so at all but, quite deliberately, Fraser had determined to make no further contact, wanting her to make the first move.

'Well, we're going to a party tonight. It's all arranged. You'll wear black tie. Everyone, but everyone, will be there.' It was her favourite expression.

'Everyone, but everyone, will not be there. I, for one, will not be there. I, for one, will be dining at the Wig and Pen Club. There I shall meet people who give not a tinker's cuss for the type of party to which you refer.'

'I'll be round at nine o'clock. We'll have champagne at your place before we move on.' Then the line went dead. No goodbye. No chance to tell her where she could stuff her party which would be attended by the gossip press, mental notebooks at the ready, watching the behaviour of silly people being silly. Laurel had hated them too.

For a moment or two his anger was reflected in the black skies rolling overhead. He felt sticky and uncomfortably cornered, yet why? For surely he was going to—where the hell was it?—well, wherever it was, with a girl, a beautiful girl, some twelve years his junior—a girl able to pick an escort from a queue the length of the King's Road. And if she couldn't, then there was more to

Emma Fry-Cripps than he understood.

Dominated by her personality, he found a few moments later that he had, without thinking, placed champagne in the fridge, made extra ice for the occasion and rinsed out the champagne bucket.

When 9.00 p.m. came and went Bart Fraser was not in the least surprised. He knew that she would turn up in her own time, which she did, shortly after ten.

'You realize that I've got to be off early in the morning? At five-fifteen no less.' Fraser found that, without thinking, he was adopting a stern, reproachful attitude, as if subconsciously he were covering the pleasure which sight of her had brought.

As she kicked the door closed, she kissed him on the cheek as if it were the most natural thing in the world. To her it was. 'I forgot to tell you, it's fancy dress.' She looked him up and down. 'But you'll do very well as you are. There'll be nobody else there in a dinner-jacket. Especially one that old.'

'Good. Because I have no intention of changing, not for you nor for any Hooray Henry from S.W.3. Where is this party anyway?'

'It's at Bunjy's. Surely you knew that? Didn't you read the rest of my column?' As she spoke Emma mounted the stairs to the sitting-room and, following her up, Fraser suddenly became appreciative of the climb as he saw the endlessly enjoyable legs which her Drum Majorette's outfit revealed. She was wearing white cowboy-style boots, white satin panties and a navy blue tunic with a red, white and blue peaked cap.

'Where's your bugle?' he enquired.

'No bugles, but if you do the fiddling, then I'll play a pretty good tune.' If she were out to shock then she did. His eyes were quizzical, mouth half open, trying to think of a response but nothing seemed suitable. She eased the cap from her head. 'Do stop gawping, there's a good chap. You look just like a solicitor. Run and get the champagne, would you.'

By the time they reached the party it was nearly eleven. Emma had consumed most of the champagne and, for such a young head, appeared not in the least affected. Fraser too had enjoyed a glass, wishing that he could have drunk more, feeling a near uncontrollable desire to empty the bottle.

Bunjy's turned out to be a house in The Boltons which, while innocuous from the outside, contained within all the trappings of unlimited wealth: a disco, a music room, a small cinema, a swimming pool, a solarium and infinite reception rooms and bedrooms, all of which seemed to be full of that thin skim of London Society with thick heads and no chins. A plastic surgeon could have made a fortune, while a brain surgeon would have found business in short supply.

Almost physically dragging him, Emma confronted Fraser with an orgy of frenzied movement, of girls draped over chairs, of men sitting on the floor, talking about the racing prospects for the following day. But no one could have heard them and their thoughts were not worth listening to anyway.

'Ah!' Emma steered him to a grotesquely short, fat man of over fifty, who was gyrating with a candelabra on his head. 'That's Bunjy.' The man saw her and his gyrating stopped. His face, which was shaped like a deflating soccer ball, broke into a smile as he gave her a huge bear hug. He was dressed as Friar Tuck, which seemed appropriate. 'Bunjy darling,' she shouted at him, 'I want you to meet a friend. A very good friend.'

'Who is he?' he shouted back.

Fraser thrust his hand forward as Emma continued the introduction. 'Bunjy, this is Farty Braser.' She turned to Fraser. 'Farty, I want you to meet Bunjy. He really is a cuddly old dear. Or should I say cuddly old queer?'

'Nice to meet you, Farty,' said Bunjy, seeming not in the least surprised at the unusual name which Fraser's parents had apparently given him. He then turned away to continue his solitary gyrating, leaving the solicitor very self-conscious, alone in the middle of the room, with Emma nowhere to be seen. He helped himself to Bucks Fizz, felt better for it and even better after the second. As he stood sipping and looking round him, the twelve-year barrier seemed unbridgeable. Had he ever really been like that? Surely the answer was no, though Bunjy had bridged the gap, despite his age. But then Bunjy didn't mind cavorting like a dervish in the hope of attracting a catamite for the night.

Most of the food had gone. Someone had stubbed out a cigarette in the middle of the Boar's Head. The tail from someone's lion outfit was draped across the remains of the smoked salmon. Suddenly Fraser no longer felt hungry, no longer felt able to stay a moment longer. It was all absurd and anyway where the hell was Emma? He picked his way through the downstairs, looking everywhere for her, being careful to step over a man in a space suit who was successfully enticing an attractive young zebra to divest herself of her stripes.

Outside there was fresh air, sanity and a taxi. 'Belgravia Mews, please. I've just been at a place called Bunjy's. Know anything about him?'

'A great big poofter. Works as a middle man for the Arabs. Rich as hell.'

'I left early.'

'Nobody else will. Parties there always go on all night. Least, that's what they say. It's not good for our business.'

In the peace of his own room, he sprawled on a sofa. For how long he rested he was unsure. The sound of a taxi stopping and the echo of a knocker forced him to his feet. It was Emma, looking as fresh as ever, saluting with one arm and carrying a basket of goodies in the other.

Without waiting for an invitation, she was inside and climbing the stairs.

'Champers, compliments of Bunjy. Pop it in the fridge. And there's a few other bits and pieces I took too.' So saying, she draped herself sideways across an armchair, leaving a somewhat bemused Fraser clutching bottle and basket. 'Phew, I'm bushed, but then it was that sort of party. Picked up just what I was after.'

Fraser hopped from foot to foot, rather expecting some word of explantion or apology but none came. 'Don't you think you owe me some word of explanation?' The narrowing of the eyes and the downturn in his voice showed his annoyance.

'Don't look so cross, Barty. It makes you even more good-looking than ever.' She laughed loudly and with an extravagant heave of her left leg, pulled off one boot, rapidly followed by the other. 'That's better.' She smiled at him for a moment. 'Well, go on. Don't just stand there like a dreary solicitor about to read out a will. Do something.'

Fraser turned on his heel. There was no answer to this extraordinary girl. And what were her intentions? Certainly dishonourable by the look of her. And what did that mean to him? He wasn't sure. 'You realize I'm leaving early in the morning, don't you? I can't stay up all night.'

'Pity. I like a stayer,' she answered ambiguously, 'but I for one have no intention of staying up all night. I've been working hard this evening, so don't be such an old hen. If Barty's a good boy he can and will have four hours' sleep.' Fraser heard a clump as she threw a boot across the room and, when he rejoined her, Fraser found that she had unleashed her hair from beneath the majorette's cap so that it now flowed freely. He doubted if he'd seen anything so obviously promiscuous since the nympho at the Sandhurst June Ball. 'Going to France for fun?' she enquired.

'France is always fun.'

'That's not an answer. I mean, are you working? Or can I come with you?'

'You! Come with me? No way.'

'So you're working?'

'I didn't say that.'

'But you are, none the less.'

'Sort of.'

'Well then, why can't I come?'

'I don't know. I hadn't thought about it. Why should you want to come?'

'I like the Burgundy country.'

Knowing that he'd never mentioned his destination, Fraser's face gave away his surprise at her comment. Did she know something? He was uncertain. 'You like it, do you?'

'Yes. You should get good weather at Beaune.' All the while her expressive, dancing eyes were enjoying themselves. She revelled in the role of puppet-master, loved being in the know. It was her stock in trade. 'I can't wait any longer for that champagne.'

Bart Fraser was relieved to have a moment alone in the kitchen, trying to assess just what was going on. 'You fancy yourself as a clairvoyant?' he enquired as he returned, handing her the delicate tulip-shaped glass brimming with Bunjy's champagne.

'Facts. That the world I live in.' She sipped the champagne. 'Bunjy must be on an economy drive — not one of his better bottles. But it'll do. Oh! do come and sit down. Stop hovering. I'm not going to eat you. Yet.' She motioned him into her chair and draped herself across his lap, one arm round his neck, the other stroking his cheek. 'I did well tonight at Bunjy's. The Editor sent me specially. You probably didn't see her but Erica Phœbe was there, and she's running a libel action against our paper. I just *had* to get something on her. And I did. I expect the action will settle now.'

'Was she the zebra?'

'No. She was the topless mermaid.'

'Was she? Unforgettable, I'm sure. No, I didn't see her.'

'She was upstairs—inevitable for a small-time actress on the make. I expect her manager put her up to the litigation. Wanted the publicity.' As she was talking, the short but slender fingers of her left hand were running up and down his shirt front. Intensely aware of her presence and of the mind-bending pressure which she was exerting, Fraser found himself holding her even tighter, excited by this wayward girl whose hair brushed against him, who seemed to move her body fractionally here, fractionally there, but all the time arousing his interest.

He downed his champagne and knew that everything would be all right, so different from the limp failure with the hired blonde, smelling of cigarettes, booze and the man who had just had her before. There was a barrier to go through, a barrier which had to be burst, the last, almost physical block from the days of his marriage had to be beaten and, as he noticed Emma's hand slipping inside his shirt, he knew that it was time to lay girl and ghost at the same time.

He didn't deceive himself that Emma really cared about him, for she had proved that she cared only for herself, but so long as he could pleasure her, she would be happy. 'Let's have the rest of the champagne in bed, shall we?' It could have been Emma talking but this time it wasn't, for he'd taken the initiative and for a moment it was she who looked surprised.

'OK.' A flicker of the eyes and a twitch of the gentle mouth were her answer as she eased from his lap. 'You carry me. I'll carry the champagne. No need for glasses.'

*

Bathed in the afterglow of climax, they lay entwined, luxuriating in the stillness after the frenzy of what had been. With him, he had brought the fervent intensity of two years' waiting; with her, she had brought the lusty enthusiasm which her previous behaviour had promised and the electric result had surprised them both, not least because she'd expected to dominate the moment.

The quietness of the room was broken only by the occasional creaking of ancient beams as they adjusted to the falling temperatures and the downpour at dusk. 'You've done that before,' he whispered, his mouth nuzzling into the fold of her neck.

'And I'm going to do it again. Pretty soon too. Did you say that you worked in a zoo?' She stretched an arm in the darkness for the champagne and introduced the icy green bottle with much shrieking and laughter.

'Do you realize I've got to be up in three and a half hours? I must get the early boat?'

'Why so pressing? Let's stay here for—oh, I don't know—days.'

'Because you've got an editor. I've got a client.'

'But Giles le Breton won't mind.'

'Who mentioned Giles le Breton?'

'Well, you're going to France. I've made one or two enquiries since we last met and I understand that the affidavit sworn by your former partners says you're acting for Giles le Breton. Giles le Breton has connections in Beaune. So that's where you're going. End of story.'

'Whoever my client is, I'm catching the early boat.'

'And I want to come too.'

'There's no story.'

'I'd like to come.'

'No. What I'm doing is absolutely confidential.'

'Tell me, Barty.' She was on the move again, inching her body as imperceptibly as a black mamba but equally as menacing and hypnotic. But despite the champagne, despite the obvious seduction, Fraser resisted, recalling the last time he had felt those movements. It smacked of a ploy, of a carnal scheme and he felt uneasy, almost guilty at distrusting her, but there it was again, that hand, touchtyping its way down his chest towards his loins. It was preferable to further questioning and so, turning slowly, he moved the bottle to the bedside and forced her head to the pillow with a lingering, searching kiss. If she were exploitable, then why not exploit?

The silver BMW sped unimpeded down the A.20 through Lewisham and on towards the Swanley by-pass. From the other direction came the occasional car, but in the early morning light he was able to make rapid progress and the empty roads gave him time to recollect the extraordinary events of the night.

In the clear light of dawn, with the sun rising ahead of him, the doubts which he had felt about Emma, seemed almost bizarre. Had she been sent to find out what he was doing? And for what reason? To get at Giles le Breton? Or at him? But he'd avoided her questions. The second love-making had been slower, more appreciative, and when at last it had all been over, he had been amazed to discover that Emma sometimes slept. Within seconds, the rhythmic breathing told its own story.

Scarcely daring to move, for fear of waking her, he'd forced himself to get up and had stood beside the bed, gazing at the peaceful face, trying to assess the meaning of what had occurred before covering her and taking a shower.

He'd taken out his le Breton files and gone through them again, waiting for the time to go. On impulse he wrote her a note but didn't like it, so he wrote another and better one. Then, gathering up his documents, he'd slipped them into a perspex folder and returned them to his case. 5.15 a.m. Time to leave. He'd propped the note against the remains of the champagne, kissed her gently and left.


# DALLAS, TEXAS

Hermann Kressin had been well briefed: go to McMac's. Buy a few odd things and half a dozen bottles of the Bourgogne Rouge, making sure to keep a receipt. A friend would witness the bottle being opened and jointly they would alert the Authorities that the wine didn't seem to match its label.

Easy money, he decided as he parked his Oldsmobile in Row N, Lot 38 of the gigantic car park. The temperature was just clipping 105 degrees and within a few paces his clothing was soaked by the effort of existing, let alone walking. The glare of the sun from the roofs of the hundreds of other cars dazzled him with mirror-like flashes of blinding intensity. The tarmac beneath his feet was treacly, the noise from the outside speakers of the supermarket was unpleasantly loud, blasting him with mindless rock music.

With leisurely pace he covered the first 300 yards of his 400-yard journey, head bowed, hands in the pockets of his beige canvas trousers, concerned yet unconcerned. He had not noticed the Toyota which had followed him into the park and was now cruising slowly along Row A, until it stopped directly between him and the supermarket entrance.

Its solitary occupant was a short Texan with close-cropped hair, most of which was hidden beneath a large cowboy-style hat. His left elbow was on the window-sill, his hand casually draped on the wheel. His right hand was out of sight. He waited until Kressin was about twenty feet away and slightly in front of him and then he called out. 'Hey! Which way for the airport?' By now he was leaning out of the window, round face smiling and friendly, every bit the stranger in distress.

Without a moment's hesitation, Kressin changed direction and approached the car. 'Sure. You got a map? I'll show you.' This exchange of words brought him right up beside the door of the driver, whose face was boyish, his cheeks almost rosy and showing no sign that they'd ever been shaved. It was a friendly face, ideal for asking the way.

The driver rummaged in the gap between the front seats. 'I've got a map here somewhere,' and all the while Kressin peered in expectantly, awaiting the chance to be helpful, tapping his foot. Suddenly the man's hand reappeared with a sharp movement and in it was a black revolver with silencer. There was no preamble. The trigger was squeezed and the bullet hit Kressin slightly to the right of centre of his forehead. The hole was neat as the bullet struck from less than 12 inch range. After smashing the roof of the skull, the exit hole was near the crown on the right-hand side, leaving behind pulped brain and lethal destruction.

In the blare of music from the loudspeakers fifty yards away the noise of the shot was muffled, and barely had the body hit the ground, partly between two other stationary vehicles, than the Toyota was cruising away without haste, without attracting attention. In thirty seconds it was on the highway, heading downtown for abandonment in a quiet street. The driver was unaware of any witness. There had been a woman with a pram but that was why he had fumbled so long, apparently searching for the map. In the lull, with no one close at hand, he'd struck. 450 easy bucks. All he needed now was the pay-off.

# LONDON

When Emma stirred and woke, realizing that she was alone, Bart Fraser had cleared Passport Control and was on the boat. 'Barty?' The voice was parched and the call half-hearted, for she knew there would be no answer. But the hope in her voice was real enough. Awaking in a strange bed was not a new experience but it took a few minutes to make out her surroundings in the thick darkness of the heavily draped room.

When she found the light switch, she blinked at the intrusion and then saw the note which she read. The handwriting was bold and forceful, much in the character of the lover of the night before.

> Sorry to 'Beat the Retreat' but this drum major has a gammy leg. Keeping pace with you for another encore might have brought shame on the Regiment. Maybe we shall meet again? If you want me, then I'm at the Hotel de la Poste at Beaune. You seem so well informed that I won't bother to give you the telephone number; you probably know it. You probably even know the number of the room I shall be using. Your offer to come was tempting but you ask too many questions. That's *my* job. I shall miss you — you're fun. Yours affectionately. Bart. PS. There are beans in the fridge.

The tenor of the note surprised her, reflecting as it did several sides of his complex character. Sides which, despite her questions, she had failed to discover. Indolently she swung her naked body out of bed, crushing her majorette's hat as she did so. It typified the start to the day, but half an hour later she had bathed and was back in the outfit, including the crumpled cap. Ignoring the invitation to eat the beans, she sat at his small table with toast, coffee and orange juice.

Surrounding her was all manner of clutter: yesterday's newspaper, some law books, his Practising Certificate and any number of old files and scribbling pads. Idly she flicked open a large blue notepad and, as she sipped the coffee, she turned through the pages, not making much sense of most of his jottings written in the same assertive style as he had displayed in bed.

Most of the notes were hastily scribbled, much altered and highly technical. It was clearly a book where he drafted notes and ideas, balanced his judgment. It was only when she saw 'G. le B' that she knew that the notes were about Giles le Breton. She read on avidly, struggling harder now to decipher Fraser's own style of self-reminding notes. By the time she had finished, her coffee was cold but her mind was hot.


## SAVANNAH, GEORGIA

An unattractive sight, Joe Mocari was sprawled across his hotel bed. He was bloated from a good lunch with plenty of pasta and, dressed only in boxer shorts, the hairy rolls of stomach rose and fell as, heavy with jug wine, he slept away the heat of the afternoon. When the telephone rang, it was an age before he answered. It was Nat Coburn. 'That sure was some shut-eye you were having, Joe.' A grunt was the only reply, so Coburn continued. 'I've good news and bad news. I'm coming in.'

Again there was a grunt. Joe's head was fuzzy, his tongue furry, his limbs stiff and disorientated. He stood by the bed and stretched out but on seeing his profile in the mirror, he turned away, preferring not to see the mess which he had made of his body.

The knock on the door announced Coburn's arrival. 'You want to lose some of that flab. Otherwise you ain't goin' to live to enjoy all this dough we're goin' to make,' Coburn said, giving Mocari a friendly punch in the midriff.

Joe Mocari was in no mood for banter. 'It had better be urgent. I don't like being woken up. Now, if you'll excuse me, I'll take a shower. When I come out, we'll talk.'

Coburn was unabashed. 'Sure. I'll help myself to some Scotch. You carry on. Get that lousy red wine washed right out of you.' The Californian stood by the picture window, looking across at the berths whitened by clouds of kaolin for export, and at the small cargo ship shrouded in white mist as loading continued.

Mocari reappeared, the remains of his hair tousled. 'Sorry, Nat. I guess I was a bit hard on you.'

'As fat slobs go, you'll do. Forget it, Joe.' Coburn eyed the New Yorker with some disapproval. 'I'll give you the bad news first. Kressin's dead. Shot outside McMac's.' Coburn's ungenerous eyes and mouth were at their meanest as he spoke. He was putting Mocari under pressure, confident that Mocari knew.

'Well, I guess Dallas is a pretty rough place. But it sure seems some kinda coincidence to me.' Mocari's own eyes were on the move, seeking shelter from the steadfast enquiry posed by Coburn.

'No coincidence, Joe. Like, I mean he wasn't mugged. No theft. Just a single bullet.'

'Had he been in McMac's? Bought the wine?'

'You tell me, Joe. I don't know.'

Mocari started slightly. 'What do you mean by that?'

'Oh, nothing, Joe. Just a kinda figure of speech.'

'Right. Only don't go suggesting I know anything about it. I know nothing.' Mocari drained the rest of his beer from the can. 'So that's the bad news. What can be good?'

'I'd set up another man. In Georgetown. He went into McMac's just like Kressin was going to do. He's now lodged a complaint with the Regional Administrator at the Bureau of Alcohol, Tobacco and Firearms in Philadelphia, as well as the US Customs in Washington.'

'What did he say?' Mocari did not sound over-enthusiastic.

'Told them the wine was rubbish and not French at all, even although it had Appellation Contrôlée stamped all over the label.'

'And?'

'And the authorities are taking it seriously. So it's time to broadside. Agreed?'

'Agreed.' Mocari tried to look happy. Making monkeys out of McMac was a cheap form of suicide. Someone else paid for your bullet.

'Great news, huh?' said Coburn again. 'Let's celebrate at the Pink House.' He could understand Joe's fear of the men behind Senator Janus and his desperate attempt to save his own neck by protecting McMac. So he'd let it ride, leave Joe twisting slowly over the heat of the grill, never knowing just how much Coburn knew.

Mocari looked up. 'But, heh! I didn't know nothing about a second man set up in Georgetown.'

Coburn smiled. 'No. Just an idea I had. I reckoned that Dallas was the wrong place anyway. We were better to go for the East Coast society. They're the great wine-drinkers. Think they know a thing or two about it. And Georgetown's full of the Washington intelligentsia, full of reporters. Boy, when this story breaks overnight it's sure goin' to travel fast, and every bottle, every one of the three million on McMac's shelves, will have to be called in. Joe, no blue-skying: we've hit the big one real hard and those Frenchies are gonna be squealin' before the week's out.'

'You're right, Nat, but, shit, I guess we should have

avoided McMac. We'd better find out what happened to Kressin.'

Coburn smiled but said nothing.

## BEAUNE

The early-morning cleaner scrubbing the step outside the Hotel de la Poste wiped her nose on her sleeve. Then she shook her head in amazement, for it was a rare sight to see a guest appearing at 6.00 a.m., dressed in tracksuit and bobble hat. Couldn't have made the best of the hotel's food and cellar last night, she determined. But she was wrong, for Bartholomew Fraser had dined exceptionally well and had drunk even better, though careful to avoid quantity. In the tranquillity of the early morning he had found getting up no problem and had proceeded to shake the ancient hotel with a few squat thrusts and some press-ups as a warm-up routine.

'Le jogging,' he muttered at the staring woman, who responded with another wipe of the nose, only this time in the other direction. The previous morning he had been driving through the scruffy hinterland of Greater London. By lunch-time he had survived the Boulevard Périphérique around Paris before joining the Autoroute for the last 200 miles to Beaune. Though it had been uneventful, he had arrived exhausted, glad to get off the busy road, his eyes leaden through lack of sleep.

He'd decided to lap the Ramparts before the Boulevards were filled with their usual stream of lorries, thundering north, south, east and west through the small town, which its mayor had described as the 'navel of Europe'. He knew that Beaune was a jewel of a town, with 16,000 inhabitants, its hard centre ringed by the ancient Ramparts, dating from Medieval times. It was an ideal place for jogging, he quickly decided, as he moved from one Boulevard to the next, every turn bringing a different view of the centre, amazingly unspoilt by the ravages of time and war. It was like returning to stay in the house of an old friend, for nothing had changed but himself, or so it appeared. As a Master of Wine he'd been coming to Beaune for fifteen years and there was scarcely a cellar which he had not visited in this, the centre of the Burgundy trade, the home of the négociants whose reputations were second to none but whose integrity occasionally provided shelter for the unscrupulous.

A slight detour down the Rue d'Alsace led him through the Place Carnot and on past the Hôtel Dieu. It was worthy of the detour, despite his flagging legs, for the ancient Hospice with its slated roof in multi-coloured patterns was unique in his experience. Beneath the cobbled streets were cellars, endlessly twisting, turning, burrowing, rising, falling, widening, narrowing, all filled with the inheritance of their past and worth a fortune too. Yet possibly here, in their midst, was one man so callous, so daring and so dishonest as to fob off inferior plonk as the finest Chambertin.

Gasping for breath as he forced himself to keep moving over the last fifty yards, he was thankful that the hotel had a lift. It would have been undignified to collapse in Reception. The girl at the desk was talking to the cleaner and their heads turned as Fraser stumbled across in front of them but all he heard was laughter and someone muttering something about '*les foux anglais*'.

## LONDON

Giles le Breton was alone in his home in Wellington Road. From his bedroom window he looked out across

Lord's Cricket Ground and could see the dew glinting in the morning sun. He never breakfasted, preferring always, whatever the weather, to walk either along the banks of the Regent's Canal or to go into the Park, where he had a nodding acquaintance with dog-walkers, strollers and a handful of joggers. But violent exercise was not for him. He preferred to take in the day at its own pace and this morning was certainly a day for the most gentle of strolls.

He passed the Wellington Hospital which he assumed to be as full of Arabs and the international rich as usual. A week ago, or was it a month ago, or a hundred years ago, he had been happy and a walk on a morning such as this would have set him up for the day. There would have been a spring in his step, a flower in his buttonhole, an expansive smile for all he met. But the knowledge that someone had struck at his business and might strike again was a daily depressant. He followed his usual route, crossing the Canal, down to Queen Mary's Gardens and then back down the Broad Walk to the Canal by Prince Albert Road. There, as always, he bought his morning paper.

' 'Morning, guv,' said the newsagent, handing across *The Times* as usual.

' 'Morning. Beautiful, isn't it?' Giles le Breton was about to turn away when a story on the front of the *Daily Telegraph* caught his eye. A glance at the bolder headlines of the *Daily Mail* and *Daily Express* revealed different stories. 'I'll take one of each of them today.' He pointed at the entire range of daily papers and then, laden down with the bundle of newsprint, hurried back to his sixth-floor apartment. As he got in the door he heard the telephone ringing.

'Giles le Breton,' he said.

' 'Morning. My name is Bill Rhodes. I'm a freelance journalist. I was just reading the morning papers. Do you have any comment?'

'What do you mean?' Giles le Breton sounded unconcerned.

'About this Chambertin. You must know what it's all about. At L'Esprit restaurant. Reading between the lines, it looks as though some of your company's top of the market wine was rubbish. Do you have any comment?'

'No. None at all.' Giles le Breton put down the phone. Within seconds it started to ring again, so he took it off the cradle and broke off the connection. He had some reading to do.

Suddenly, the day didn't seem sunny any more, the birds had stopped singing as he stooped forward to study the papers. *The Times* did not carry the story but the *Telegraph, Mail, Topic, Express, Sun* and *Mirror* had splashed the tale.

Slowly he walked to the balcony and stared across at the restful green expanse of the world's most famous cricket ground. He could remember so many great occasions there and to see the imperious outline of the pavilion, with the windows of the Long Room just visible, was enough to bring them back. But now, this morning, he thought only of the smears and innuendo which had ripped the heart from his business. There had been no hint of what was coming. Who had broken the story? Presumably someone at L'Esprit, but whoever it was had fed slanted material, casting slurs on the French and on his Company in large measures. He personally was roundly criticized for the cover-up, but Marjorie Harley, who knew the truth, had declined to comment.

He thought of the vast stocks of wine coolly lying side by side at St James's. Were they real? Were they what they were supposed to be? Apparently yes, but if *he* were unsure, then how would the world and everyone know? At a stroke their value was in doubt. The bank would be inviting him to call in to discuss the position — of that he had no doubt. Overdrafts would be reviewed, buying power reduced, cash flow in jeopardy.

And young Angelo, the boy from Italy whom he had befriended, had gone back to Rome. It had been a discreet yet loving relationship. They had met in Florence while he'd been negotiating with some Chianti dealers. Angelo had been a student and their friendship had developed into an invitation to come and stay in London. But Angelo had tired of the arrangement, adding yet another crushing burden on top of so much else. The youth had been an intimate confidant and a ready listener, but he was bored with the secrecy and the problems under which Giles was labouring. Despite pleas for him to stay, Angelo had gone and the parting had been bitter and resentful.

Giles's affection and respect for Barty Fraser were kept in a different pigeonhole and, despite their near lifelong friendship, he was not the person to whom he could turn to discuss the aching miss of the love of an Italian boy, with dark brown eyes, olive skin and firm yet gentle limbs.

He was alone.

The tears welled in his eyes as he returned to his sitting-room. A French clock gave a gentle reminder that it was nine o'clock and that he was late for work. He ignored it, knowing that he was in no state to face the barrage of questions from employees, the Press, his shareholders and other directors. There would have to be a meeting of the Board, a crisis meeting of shareholders, explanations, apologies and yet more explanations, all sounding seemingly thinner with repetition. He longed for the advice of Bartholomew Fraser who, even in his own moments of depression, had vision and judgment founded on the rock of good sense. But he was in France. And Angelo was in Rome.

# BEAUNE

As Bartholomew Fraser saw Lucien Lubeau coming
towards him, he hoped that Lucien would shake his hand
rather than get carried away in an excess of amicable
exuberance, for the Frenchman was scarcely the kissable
type. Aged fifty-nine, with a scruffy beard and shiningly
bald head, he was only five foot seven and overweight,
with roll upon roll of excessive flesh on torso and limbs
alike.

'Bart!' The Frenchman came very close and, for a
moment, Fraser faced the prospect of the three kiss
routine with British aplomb. But the moment passed and
he was into the pumping handshake instead. Lubeau had
lived all his life in Beaune and was a member of the
Chevaliers de Tastevin. In other words he knew the
history of every vine root from Dijon to Mâcon; he knew
every nuance of every inch of invaluable soil. Above all,
he knew the good, the bad and the crooked.

After ordering large black coffees and a Cognac for
Lubeau the two men settled down, clearing the small talk
before Fraser steered the conversation in the required
direction. Lubeau's English was non-existent, so Fraser
spoke in French, which presented no problem, for while
with Bream and Bream he'd made use of his fluency in
Italian, German and French to the advantage of those of
his partners whose knowledge seemed to run only as far as
opening time or the date of the Derby. 'The matters of
which I am going to speak are utterly confidential. I think
you understand?'

'I do.' Lubeau looked around in a furtively theatrical
manner.

'I'm interested in Chambertin.'

The Frenchman gave no reaction whatsoever. The gaze was steady and unenquiring. 'Yes?'

'I'm not talking now of Gevrey Chambertin or of anything other than the great Chambertin itself.' Fraser waited for the man to react but again Lubeau seemed almost uninterested, his hooded eyelids drooping down. Inside his dark suit and roll-neck pullover, the jelly-like body was still. 'Are you aware of any trouble here in Beaune among your great shippers? With Chambertin, I mean.'

'No.' The response was immediate and dismissive. 'Nothing. Sometimes I hear shippers do this or that to improve taste or, more likely, profitability. Sometimes — yes, a company's integrity is questioned.' The small eyes narrowed beneath bushy brows. 'This is unquestionably the world centre of fine wines.' He knew that Fraser thought that Bordeaux held the crown. 'We have to stamp out the unscrupulous.'

'But the opportunities must still exist. Take a company like Gustave Furneaux, who supplied le Breton & Co. in England.'

'Oh yes, and inevitably so, for history has decreed that our wines, even the great Chambertin, can be a blend from any number of growers. That's the difference between here and Bordeaux. So maybe the unscrupulous *stretch* their good wines with a lesser product, coming not from the true vineyard at all. Time was when truckloads of Algerian wine arrived to *stretch* the wine — or perhaps to improve it by giving added body to a thin vintage.'

'But what about the French authorities? Can they be relied upon?'

The Frenchman laughed. 'The people in the Department called "Oppression de Fraud" are conscientious. But you know the Gallic touch? Our hatred of authority. Our *disdain* for authority. Rules are there to be transgressed, whether for no overtaking before a dangerous bend or for the way we blend our wines. The temptation for easy profit, when banks are pressing, has led even the occasional blue chip to take a chance. But as for Gustave Furneaux & Co?' He shook his head, laid his hands across his ample stomach and coughed with some sign of distress. 'No. *Pas possible*. Financially they're very sound. You'll have to look somewhere else.'

'I'm touring their cellars this afternoon. Why not come with me? You might just spot something that I miss.'

'All right. I'd enjoy that.'

'Meet me here at three, then. That's unless you care to join me for lunch?'

'Sorry, but I'm meeting my accountant.'


# BEAUNE

'Can I talk to Roger Talbooth, please?' Bartholomew Fraser had just got through to his solicitors.

'Is that you, BF?' Talbooth had always persisted with the abbreviation, dating back to their days at Oxford.

'Yes. Any developments?'

'Yes and no. Nothing involving Bream's, but I'm sorry to say that you've just lost a client.' Talbooth was unsure what to say, not knowing what, if anything, his listener had heard.

'What do you mean?' Fraser's voice gave away that he knew nothing.

'Giles le Breton has been found dead this morning. Neighbours heard a single shot.'

'Murdered?'

'Unlikely.'

'Why?'

'Because of the morning papers. Full of stuff about some duff Chambertin which his firm had shipped, though to my way of thinking they were blaming the French for some neat sleight of hand.'

'How the hell did the Press pick it up?' Fraser was thinking aloud, forgetting that his listener knew nothing of the true story of the Chambertin.

'I'm sorry, I missed that.'

'Oh, nothing. But it's scarcely credible. And yet, having said it, I can see that it is. Giles was never a happy man. I suppose it could be suicide.' The depth of the shock was still shallow, perhaps because of distance, perhaps because it was second-hand. Either way, it was unreal. A moment or two before he'd been looking forward to his lunch. Now everything had changed. 'I'll come back. I'm one of his executors.' His client, his *only* client, was dead, for only he and Giles had known of his precise role. Now the story of the restaurant was known.

'What about the Bream case?'

'No change. I'm retained by the company though I've only worked for Giles personally.'

'So you want me to continue with the litigation?'

'Yes. We fight all the way. The principle remains the same. 'Bye.'

The solicitor stared into the endless blue sky. The rest of the world was shut out. The only image which formed and re-formed was of a shotgun and of a crumpled figure. Giles le Breton. A man who was as staunch a friend as you could get, a man of irreproachable honesty who had felt the need to destroy himself because of a story splashed by a handful of journalists who cared not whom they besmirched, whom they smeared with unfair innuendoes. The great dragon called *copy* had been fed for another day.

Thoughts of journalists reminded him of Emma. A flicker of doubt crossed his mind, which he tried to dismiss without success. Had he said anything to her? Had he given away any secret? But no. He was confident that he had said nothing, given nothing away which could have given her a story to syndicate to the rest of Fleet Street.

He felt no need to lunch, for his stomach was tight and drawn. In different circumstances the tantalizing smell and clatter of plates from the dining-room would have proved irresistible, but he barely noticed either as he walked through Reception, automaton-like, into the welcoming hot midday air. Remembering nothing of the route which he took, he found himself drawn irresistibly towards the Jardin Anglais at the other side of the city. The beauty of the trees, of the grass, of the birdsong and of the sunlight was such that happiness seemed indecent and he found himself fighting against his emotions until their inevitable victory. With no one else around, in the shadiness of a quiet corner, he lay down and whimpered and sobbed like a heartbroken child.

Keeping his appointment at the offices of Gustave Furneaux was an effort but he'd decided that he must, that the probing must continue. It wasn't made easier by Lucien Lubeau's small talk, jokes and laughter, until at last he felt he had to tell him about Giles. Uppermost in his mind was his failure. If he'd discovered the source of the deception, then undoubtedly Giles would still have been alive. It was his fault, yet it determined him the more to press on for vengeance.

'And this is where you are blending your wines, is it?' Fraser enquired of the guide. It was a conversational remark, for Fraser knew full well exactly what was happening in the high-vaulted room.

'Yes. Here we are seeking to blend the wines from three different vineyards from which we have purchased. The end result will be the perfection which we expect.'

'And you strive for the same balance of flavour and colour every year?'

'Yes. We always try to achieve the same end result,

which is to blend the wines from the different vineyards of the same Appellation into the style of our own House. People who buy from us, recognizing our label, will know the style of wine which they will get. They know that our Volnay will be paler than most but still rich in after-taste. They could go to another shipper and purchase a Volnay which would be entirely different, yet nevertheless very fine.'

'And at the other end of the market? The bulk end?'

'We still aim to enhance the reputation of our company.'

'But what about slipping in the occasional vat of Algerian wine, or something from the deep South?'

'*Stretching* the wine!' The guide's laugh was incredulous and slightly admonishing. 'It may happen elsewhere. But here? Here, you are in the cellars of one of the most prestigious négociants in the world. We would never attempt any such thing. Our business is too successful and our reputation too great, and there's the Fraud Squad for the wine trade which comes under the Ministry of Agriculture. They can descend like predators and check our records, check our wines, count our stock, take samples and—' he shrugged his shoulders before continuing—'send us to prison.'

'But still this type of fraud goes on from Beaune?'

'Perhaps. There were troubles, for example, in 1973. Some négociants had been over-sugaring their Beaujolais—a fact which was discovered by the authorities. And there were prosecutions. You can only add sugar in strictly controlled circumstances, after proper notice to the authorities. I expect you know that?'

Fraser nodded. 'But could your bottom of the market wine get wrongly labelled and be sent out as best Chambertin?'

'No. Absolutely not.'

'What about bottling?'

'Some goes to Holland and America in bulk but the best is always bottled here, when we're satisfied that fermentation has finished. The process from the arrival of the crude, rough wine from the vigneron to the end product is a long and skilled one. We have to rack the wine, place it in clean casks, check for cloudiness, rack the wine again, top up the casks until at last the moment for bottling has arrived.'

Fraser persisted. 'What about one wine becoming confused with a different wine of a different quality?'

'Impossible. All the casks are labelled, all the records are kept. We have so many visitors, so many bureaucrats, so much form-filling, that the chance of a mistake can be ignored.'

Of course Fraser understood that the guide was putting out the official party line; nevertheless he was convinced of the good sense of the explanations given. No one could get away with fraud for very long.

'The English papers today have a story involving one of your wines.' Both guide and Lucien Lubeau looked sharply at Fraser as he now stood, casually leaning against a massive vat. 'Apparently some of your Chambertin, imported by Giles le Breton, from these very cellars, bears no resemblance to Chambertin whatsoever. Indeed, there were suggestions that the wine probably came from Italy.'

'I have no comment to make. I know nothing of this. I would just say it is—impossible.' The guide was visibly shaken as they came into the broad sunlight of the yard and skirted round a container lorry which was being loaded with cases of wine. 'Come in here.' The guide led the way. 'We have one or two interesting wines for you to sample in the Hospitality Room.'

# LONDON

Fraser's taxi made swift progress into the West End from Heathrow. He'd left his car in France, preferring to take the quickest route, anxious to learn the worst about the death of Giles le Breton. As the taxi entered the elevated section over Chiswick, his tiredness and depression kept telling him that the trip had been a waste of time when, on the contrary, he knew that the trip had been successful, if only to prove a negative.

For all the breezy confidence of the guide, Fraser was convinced that no system was foolproof, that the biggest deterrent to fraud was reputation rather than any other single expedient.

As the Airbus had circled over the lights of London, he'd mused that the burden of proof was not dissimilar to that for adultery — it was insufficient to prove inclination; insufficient to prove opportunity. Essential to prove *both* before a Judge would find the case proven. So with the Chambertin, while opportunities existed, inclination was lacking. A dawn raid by the French Fraud Squad with 100 bottles received, 120 bottles in stock, was a formula for instant profit but a short fuse for discovery.

But had Giles discovered something, heard something, clinching the guilt of his own company? Unlikely, but not something to be dismissed. The evening paper splashed the death. Foul play was not suspected. A neighbour described finding le Breton lying on his back with a twelve-bore shotgun across his legs, still gripped by the muzzle in his left hand. The image was unpleasant and haunting.

There were quotations from other wine-shippers, using guarded tones, mainly referring to the respect in which

Giles had been held in the trade. Nevertheless the reporter had not missed the connection with the cover-up of the Chambertin fraud. Good copy for the Press but bad news for a long-standing friendship; bad news for the solicitor whose only client had been found lying on his back with a twelve-bore shotgun gripped near the muzzle by the left hand. The image repeated itself, the obsession remained.

Inside his cottage, the memories of his departure flooded back. The squashed cap of a Drum Majorette caught his eye but otherwise the sitting-room was normal and, in the bedroom, everything was neat. But for the cap, it was as if Emma had never been there at all.

No—not quite, he decided. There were the crumbs of her breakfast beside his notebook on the table. A tremor went through him as he recalled the contents and flicked over the pages until he came to his notes of the evening at L'Esprit. The tremor stopped, to be replaced by a chill, and then by a flush which seemed to reach every part of his body at the same moment. The notes of the cover-up were full and frank and intended for himself alone, yet they were now stained by a ring from a coffee cup.

He stared at the page. It wasn't him so it had to be Emma. She had read the notes—and must have blown the story, no doubt making lots of money, while keeping her name out of it. That was Emma! Too clever, too ruthless and too amoral. Publish anything—that's what she'd said. Even if it meant the death of an innocent man.

Christ! Oh Christ! The bitch! The unscrupulous, devious little bitch!

In anger he threw his notebook to the floor. Had he looked in the mirror, he would have seen that his face had blanched, that the stubble of the day's growth was heavy and that his eyes were sagging and ready for sleep. Had he really started his day jogging round the city of Beaune? It seemed a lifetime before. And Giles had been alive then. And now he had to live with the realization that Emma, the girl with the seductive ways, had duped him, had brought about the death of Giles le Breton by her greed. Did he have to face that? For ever?

Yes.

His tread uncertain, his mind splintered with confusions, he made for the bottle of malt whisky, the special blend of A.H. le Breton & Co., Ltd. It seemed appropriate and he filled the tumbler, emptied it and filled it again.

For God's sake, why had death stalked him like this, adding a third notch to his conscience! Wife, daughter, best friend. Was that his lot? To be the death of those of whom he thought the most and who had done the most for him?

Yes.

To bring about the death of his only client?

Yes.

He didn't bother with the tumbler any more. The malt flowed easier from the bottle. Much more comforting.

Emma Fry-Cripps put down the receiver. By her standards her face was thoughtful, for it was the third time with no response from Bartholomew Fraser's number. And there had been no reply when she had visited Belgravia Mews, despite the light burning in an upstairs room; a light which she knew she had switched off on her departure.

She wasn't quite clear why she was so keen to see him. Was it because of the news which she wanted to tell him or the desire to see him once again? Maybe a bit of each, she decided as she gazed vacantly at the first draft of her piece for the next edition. While being unable to recall Barty's face, she nevertheless found the complex pastiche of his character intriguing. At one point he was the little boy lost, searching for security, shovelling desperately hard to bury his past; then, moments later, he was strong, determined and resourceful. With a slight ache in her loins she could recall the night spent together, could still feel surprised by the fervent intensity of his ardour and this despite the wasted and much scarred leg.

In the cosy, flippant world in which she moved, her lovers had always been deep-tanned perfection, with rippling muscles and empty heads. But there was more to it than sex. She *had* to see him, had so much to explain, had so much to tell him as a result of the death of Giles le Breton.

'I won't be back today,' she announced. It was her way: no explanations to her superiors, no indication what she was doing, or where, or why. But they accepted her because she picked up gossip before the remarks had been made, could read an adulterer's mind before the act had taken place. As far as the Deputy Editor was concerned that was good enough for him, particularly as she had never proved averse to his occasional improper suggestion.

Bartholomew Fraser lay on his bed. He had some recollections of undressing, of forcing himself to put aside the bottle unfinished, knowing that, despite everything, the answer to his problems lay not there but in his own resilience, yet when morning came he had slept not at all. Rather he had lain in a never-ending variety of positions, all of which were as uncomfortable as his cascading torrent of thoughts: his wife's face lacerated by the windscreen, little Katy's face unsullied, yet dead and now grotesquely defiled by a Drum Majorette's cap. A shotgun. Wine. Giles le Breton. Shotgun. Screeching brakes. The flat in Stage House. Hideous furniture. That night when he had returned home to Forest Row. The creaking emptiness of the building. The smoky fireplaces. The Drum Majorette's cap. The tranquil figure of Emma, as he had left her, naked and uniquely childlike in slumber. And the newspapers. And the treachery of her. And the shotgun, left hand near the muzzle.

He had been conscious of the brass knocker on the front door being banged incessantly, repeatedly, had heard voices from the street. Then it had been the telephone ringing, maybe once, maybe a dozen times during the morning. It had been like a stone in the shoe or a nagging toothache. He had tried to pretend that it wasn't ringing, that no one wanted him, that it would all go away and everything would be all right.

Totally exhausted, he had lain there until sleep had come around lunch-time and only now, as mid-afternoon approached, did he feel able to journey from horizontal to vertical. The bloody phone was *still* ringing. Ignoring it, he went off in search of a shower and a coffee just as Emma was leaving her desk in Fleet Street. By the time her taxi had taken her through the crowded Strand and Trafalgar Square, past Buckingham Palace, to Belgravia Mews, Fraser was feeling somewhat better. He peered out and saw at least five or six journalists, hanging about in a small group.

A taxi pulled up and out stepped Emma, deceptively virginal in white cheesecloth shirt and clinging white jeans. From where he stood, about two paces from the window, trying to keep out of sight, Fraser could feel the threat of conflicting emotions. As he saw her join the group of cigarette-smoking men on the opposite pavement, it was as if he were watching a peepshow into someone else's life. But the resonant bang on the door changed all that.

He hesitated and then, almost against his better judgment, went down. 'Come in.' His voice was brusque.

He banged the door shut as soon as she was inside. For a moment they stood in the gloom of the hall, looking at each other, she with head on one side, mouth half open, ready to respond to his advance. Then she saw his snarl of anger and her smile of friendship froze as Fraser's hand caught her a stinging blow across her right cheek, causing her to swirl round like a top. 'Bitch. Snivelling, sneaking little bitch.' Still cowering from the blow, she half looked at him from behind the crook of her protective elbow. Scarcely knowing what he was doing, Fraser grasped her arm and pulled her away from the door and up the stairs. As he saw that she was opening her mouth to scream, he stopped her with the instant command. 'Shut up! You've done enough damage already.'

The steel in his voice, the glint of hatred in his eye, killed her scream before arrival. Roughly pushing her in front of him, he forced her to sit in the chair where she had breakfasted. 'Sit down.' As soon as she had done so, he confronted her with the notebook.

'You've read this, haven't you? Been through my things for a story.' The tone of voice had changed to contempt, his face close to hers, his hand flourishing the notebook. 'Does the gutter press sink that low?' Emma's delicate pink cheeks had paled, the brimming confidence had gone. 'Why? Why did you do this to me? Are you happy? Are you happy that you've got your story and that Giles le Breton is dead? Does the fee you've earned from reading my private papers keep you in more champagne?' He threw the notebook aside, his every action coiled with nervous energy. He caught her eye, imploringly seeking explanations from the melting depths. Then he grasped her by the shoulders, shook her, as if somehow this would release answers.

'I hope the champagne tastes like blood,' he ranted as he shook her till her hair flew in all directions, her eyes tightly shut. And then he released her, his moment of anger purged. They were still and he saw her cheek now aflame with the force of the blow. Still she said nothing.

Between them was a gulf of misunderstanding and mistrust.

Choking for words and tears starting to form, Emma suddenly sprang forward and clasped herself to him. Her arms gripped round him, her head rubbing against his chest. 'Sorry, sorry, sorry, sorry, sorry.' Fraser could feel her clinging, limpet-like, to him and it was impossible not to respond. And he did so with long arms holding her to him, somehow trying to quell the sobs which reverberated throughout her. 'I'm sorry, Barty. I shouldn't have read it.' The words were punctuated with sobs. 'But I didn't, really didn't, publish the story.'

'I don't believe you.' Fraser's voice was more tender now, almost despairing, his face less black than moments before.

'It's true. It's true.' She pulled back from him and turned her head up towards his, so that he could see that she was telling the truth. The tear-stained face, the eyes calling for help and forgiveness, the mouth, always passionate and appealing, were too much.

The kiss was fervent and understanding as she forced herself upon him. 'You do believe me, don't you?' she said at last.

'I don't know why I should. But I do.'

'Shall I explain? If you give me a chance . . .'

'No. Explanations can come later.'


# NEW YORK

Outside Penn Central station it was 92 degrees and still rising. So it was that street cries seemed louder, cab horns more strident and smells more pungent than was good for man or beast. Thus thought Joe Mocari, as he glanced skywards and noticed that the morning sun had given way to a thickening layer of cloud, which would build up to a stinking, exhausting humidity by evening. But, like all New Yorkers, Joe tolerated it, for this was home, this was the place he understood, the place where, depending on his mood, he knew everybody — or knew nobody.

In the station concourse throngs of over-fired commuters sought out their Amtrak connections, but Mocari ignored the queues waiting their turn to buy tickets, or to argue with an official, which was reckoned by many to be the sport of the day. The hotter the day, the more strident the complaints about the late arrival from Boston or Philadelphia. Instead Mocari headed for the rack of newspapers which hung outside the bookstall and a glance revealed that the papers from Europe had arrived. He quickly purchased copies of *Le Figaro,* the *Daily Telegraph* and *The Times.* Then, perching himself on a counter stool in the drug store, he sipped an iced coffee and read from the English papers with obvious relish and satisfaction. The pace of the French wine scandal was accelerating and had reached front page proportions. Unable to read French, nevertheless he appreciated the gist of *Le Figaro*'s article, written under the headline CRISE EN BOURGOGNE? The article suggested that, following the initial discovery of some dubious Chablis and Volnay in Le Chameau Chambré restaurant in Paris, tests carried out within twenty-four hours, on random samples from a number of other leading restaurants had revealed more than a dozen examples of wine scattered around the city, whose contents bore no resemblance to the information on the label. 'Heads would roll' was the journalist's warning and prophecy.

In England 150,000 bottles of Chablis had been impounded at Liverpool Docks, on arrival from Holland and the English Wine Standards Board and the police were now investigating.

Joe phoned California. 'Hi! Nat! I've got the papers. Have you seen them?'

'Sure. So we go for Superblend.' This was the codename for the jackpot.

'Anything I can do?' enquired Joe. 'London's gone well. Did you read about that geyser le Breton?'

'Sure. We've done well. France, England and here with McMac's.'

'If I don't ring tomorrow, you'll know I'm dead.' Mocari wondered for a moment whether he'd been melodramatic. But, hell no. If his role in setting up the McMac affair came out, then he was expendable, certainly worth the cost of a hired hood and a solitary bullet. It was, after all, the same view that he'd taken about Kressin in Dallas, Zeeler in New York and Dupont in Paris. Death was as easy as making up your mind. A phone call, a word in the right place, and you could fix anything from New York.

Out in the sunlight he turned towards Seventh Avenue, wondering whether any decision had yet been taken on the life of Joe Mocari. It was a chilling thought.


# LONDON

'That's what I wanted to tell you,' said Emma as she climbed out of bed, her body still tingling and vibrant from the climax of love-making, her face still raw from the blow which he'd struck. Fraser watched her go, skipping naked to the doorway, and then saw her return, eyes dancing and breasts firm. As she climbed back in beside him, she was clutching a radio. 'It's almost seven o'clock in France. You do speak French, don't you?'

'*Mais oui*,' said Fraser, with a Form One accent, as she tuned in to the French News Bulletin. Then they lay, silently together, she with all the giggling excitement of someone bursting to reveal a secret, he on edge with intense curiosity at what was going on.

The major news was of a skirmish in Lebanon and the reaction of the President but, hotly behind it, came the story of growing concern in official circles at reports reaching the French Ministry of Agriculture's Fraud Squad. The whole of Burgundy was said to be a state of shock and siege, following allegations of malpractice. Dubbed the '*Affaire du Chameau Chambré*', after the restaurant where the first bogus Volnay had surfaced, the scandal had already touched the integrity of a number of Burgundy négociants. Though the media had made no connection, the wine had been part of the load carried by Claude Dupont, the driver who had died on his rounds. It was said that doubts and scepticism in the minds of the public had grown overnight as the wines of Chablis, Chambertin and Fixin had all been mentioned. Every bottle was now under suspicion. So indeed was everyone.

'There you are,' said Emma as the report ended. She sprawled across him.

'It's unbelievable. The story must have been breaking just as I was leaving France.' She felt his arms grip her strongly, tighten round her back, felt the emotion pounding through him and, as she looked up, she saw that his eyes were filling with tears. 'Poor Giles. Just twenty-four hours. If he'd waited twenty-four hours the truth would have been out, his name cleared, his future reputation restored.'

'Don't blame yourself.' It was her turn to cling to him. 'There was nothing you could do. And his problems wouldn't have gone away — not that easily.'

'But we'd have won through! The bank might have wanted further security as the value of his stock fell, but so long as the bank knew that he wasn't a party to fraud — no problem.'

'I'm sorry. He was such a good friend to you.'

'And he died for nothing. He died because some bastard framed him.' Emma could see the look on his face change, as the tears dried to be replaced by anger and determination. 'He died because he jumped to a conclusion. He died because *the world* jumped to a conclusion.'

'He's not alone in that,' Emma teased him as she manœuvred playfully across him.

'Meaning?'

'You're forgetting this already?' She pointed to the red weal on her cheek.

He fumbled for his words. 'Well, no. Well, yes. I suppose I was.' He kissed her gently on the forehead and then started to stroke her hair, as if he were calming a thoroughbred. 'I jumped to a conclusion as well, didn't I? You didn't splash the story about Giles, It wasn't you at all. The story was breaking anyway. I can see it plainly but—dear God, you do understand my mistake, don't you? You read my notes, you invaded my privacy and the story appeared immediately after.'

'You must have thought I was a right slut.'

'I did. One minute I thought that you really cared. The next? The next I thought that you had been planted by your Editor to get a scoop.' He clasped his arms around her neck so that her cheek was forced close against him, locking her eyes away from his tormented face.

'And now, what do you think now?' Emma was talking into the pillow.

'Now? About you? Just a naughty girl for looking at my notes, that's all.' He nearly went on to say that he found her the most seductive, captivating and exciting person he'd ever met but such words didn't come easily, even in the emotional state in which he found himself. He said instead: 'Is there any way I can make up for it?'

'Try me!' He stroked the nape of her neck as she pulled

back to face him, to look deep into the eyes which had avoided her.

'I've got to find out who framed Giles. And why.'

'It might be something bigger than you think.'

'I'll chance it. I've got no other clients, nothing better to do. I'll not rest, *never* rest, until I get to the bottom of it. I'd rather die than do nothing.' Bold words came easily in the cosy ambiance of the comfortable bed. At such moments danger and the permanence of death seemed a distant irrelevance. To both of them.

## MONTEREY COUNTY, CALIFORNIA

Nat Coburn spun his deep leather chair until the spotlight was perfectly angled to light his magazine. It was the first from a stack of glossies, each with a story resulting from Superblend. Karen Schunberg had done her job well. Using every contact at her disposal she had, with skill and discretion, planted enough facts for the best investigative journalists in every country to sniff the wind and to follow the scent to Beaune. Of course, her name appeared nowhere. She was simply a person with facts available and red herrings for sale, for others to apply to build their reputations. And facts coming from her were as solid and reassuring as Aunt Ethel's fruitcake.

Pausing only to pour himself a dry Martini, Coburn set in for a good read. The headline on Page 17 of *Newthink* was captivating enough after the day's work in the vineyard.

### WINEGATE REVISITED?

An air of crisis hangs shroud-like over Burgundy. Neighbours look at neighbours. Suspicion and mistrust

have replaced traditional virtues. An emergency meeting
of several leading shippers ended in disarray with
accusation and counter-accusation. The usually tranquil
city of Beaune is a hotbed of rumour and speculation. To
say there is panic would be an overstatement but those
well-placed in the grapevine confidently predict just that.

And why? The answer lies in a market which is being
increasingly flooded with dishonest wine. What started
with a suspicion in New Orleans, a doubt in Seattle and
concern in London and Paris, has deluged into a storm of
accusations against the French wine industry. Some three
million bottles of 'so-called' Bourgogne Rouge, formerly
on sale in McMac's, have been rejected by public and
distributors alike. But it's not just the bulk market, for
even the noble Chambertin has been alleged to have its
roots in Italy. Someone has been making a quick buck at
the expense of Joe Public!

When our reporter spoke to Foulshon, Frères & Cie.,
one of the leading négociants in Beaune, whose
reputation is now under threat, the response was
cautious. 'While we cannot explain why certain of our
fine wines are suspect, we nevertheless reject any
suggestion that our Company has ever supplied anything
other than wines of the highest quality. The matter is now
in the hands of the Authorities both in France and abroad
and so, until their report, we are saying nothing further.'

The temptations to make a quick buck are big enough.
A bottle of Chambertin retailing here at $60 a bottle
could have contents worth a mere $5 or less. Now,
increasingly, as people sip their élitist Burgundy, they
must be asking whether it came from Algeria, Italy or
even Greece.

The isolated reports of complaints from as far apart as
New Orleans, Chicago and Seattle gave cause for
concern. Taken in concert with the fresh revelations of
the McMac problem and a spate of revelations in Europe,

one has a crescendo of international fraud. The shadow of that multi-million-dollar fraud hangs over the French wine industry.

Already repercussions are being felt, the most tragic of which was the death in London of Giles le Breton, well respected head of the major corporation, A.H. le Breton & Co., of St James's. No inquest has taken place but it is widely accepted that le Breton blew out his brains with a shotgun shortly after reading the first reports of the scandal. Speculation that he was involved now seems wide of the mark. London solicitor, Bartholomew Fraser, was making enquiries on his behalf, following the cover-up of bogus Chambertin at L'Esprit restaurant, but Fraser has troubles of his own with an action pending against the partners in his London law firm and has been unavailable for comment.

Another story going round the gentlemen's clubs of London is that le Breton's death had nothing to do with the wine scandal at all but, rather, was to do with his discreetly homosexual life-style.

A spokesman for le Breton & Co., refused to be drawn on the financial implications of the dishonest wine bearing his company's label. With true bowler-hatted phlegm, he said: 'The tragic death of our Chairman serves as a reminder that we, at le Breton & Co., regard our name as the highest guarantee of quality. That somehow we have been duped into purchasing dishonest wine has cast the entire industry into confusion. Yes, I have heard reports that against every bottle in our cellars there now hangs a question mark. I do not propose to be drawn any further on such idle and demeaning remarks, which are so obviously false.'

To the question whether his company would reconsider its buying policy, the spokesman retorted with a brisk 'no comment.' Nevertheless, it was a fair question and one which is being increasingly asked. The protection loudly

proclaimed by the rules known as Appellation Contrôlée
has proved illusory.

Greer L. Halberstein Jr, the well-known wine
connoisseur and writer, when asked to comment from his
penthouse on New York's Upper East Side, expressed
concern for the industry as a whole. 'One often hears
stories that the French wine aristocracy, whether from
Bordeaux or Burgundy, has well-placed friends in Paris.
Stories often circulate of over-generous hospitality to
French Government officials, of strange parties with
perverts, bondage and prostitutes on tap. Certainly there
will be Ministry officials in Paris who will be anxious to
conceal their copiously filled wine cellars. The events of
the last few days have fired a salvo at Appellation
Contrôlée. My concern is that, if French growers and
dealers *are* in consort with the Ministry, then there can be
no confidence that this scandal will be investigated to its
proper conclusion.'

Students of the French wine trade will not have forgotten the Winegate scandal of 1973 when, through some
neat paper-work, the highly respected Cruse shippers of
Bordeaux beat Government controls, 'changing' white
wine into red. The ensuing prosecution kicked over the
trash can, unleashing an almighty stench of sharp
practice, but today a spokesman from Bordeaux, who
declined to be named but who is close to the
Chartronnais, told me there remains considerable
sympathy for the Cruse family, for 'they were the unlucky
ones. They got caught.'

And that is the nature of the crime as the French see it.
Haughty as Giscard d'Estaing before his downfall, thick-
skinned as General de Gaulle in his heyday, the French
aristocracy of wine have grown fat, complacent and, too
often, deceitful. Now they have been caught: not this
time in Bordeaux but instead in Burgundy.

But it would be a brave man (and not this writer for a

start) who would say that corruption in Bordeaux has been eliminated. Time only will tell. Who but the French would permit the words 'Château Bottled' to be construed as a mobile bottling plant visiting a château to carry out the procedure?

A typical example, for, while the letter of the law is maintained, the spirit is flouted and the gullible public are fooled. But every so often a crack appears and what peeps through is distinctly unpalatable and frequently undrinkable.

Meantime, the corporate importers behind McMac were reported to be contemplating legal action over the three million bottles of Bourgogne Rouge which have had to be withdrawn from the market. 'Someone will have to pay for this,' said Chief Executive Louis Spiggola from the company's headquarters in Atlantic City, which has been a hotbed of urgent meetings since the crisis arose, following complaints about the red wine from their Georgetown store.

A spokesman for the French Ministry of Agriculture, asked to comment, said it was too early to speculate on prosecutions. A number of examples of suspect wine have now reached Paris, including those from the Paris restaurants whose reputations have been damaged by the scandalous behaviour of their fellow countrymen. But then times are hard in Burgundy. Dramatically high prices have scarcely helped and the economic pressure to 'stretch' a wine by astute blending or by more flagrant abuse must not be overlooked, even though one sees few signs of penury amongst the fat cats as they cruise around Beaune in their Citroëns and Peugeots.

The world will have its eyes on the forthcoming wine auctions to take place in London and New Orleans. That prices will fall is inevitable. But those minded to speculate may be lucky. Watch this space.

★

Coburn slapped his thigh. 'Wow-ee!' he exclaimed. It was pungent stuff, more heady than even he had expected.

Karen had done well; they'd *all* done well, particularly over le Breton. It had been odd that the scandal hadn't erupted after that dinner, but even the most loyal waiters have their price and the trainee at L'Esprit had been quick to see the difference between stick and carrot.

Wisely, he'd selected the carrot. That boy could go far . . . so long as his conscience wasn't too trouble by the death of Giles le Breton.

## LONDON

'That, I didn't expect,' said Bartholomew Fraser as he joined Emma in the genial surroundings of Langan's Brasserie.

'Coincidence?' she enquired.

'I doubt it. The coroner returned an open verdict. Said that he wasn't satisfied it was suicide.'

'What was the evidence, then?'

'The driver of the tube train wasn't certain that Bragshaw deliberately jumped in front of his train. Equally, he was uncertain whether two large gentlemen standing either side of him accelerated his progress into the path of the Bakerloo line train as it came into the station. The two men disappeared and other witnesses weren't very convincing. In fact the only person at the inquest who might have swayed their views was me. But I was saying nothing, just sitting at the back, just watching what was going on.' Almost without thinking, he found that he had ordered himself a double brandy and ginger ale as an apéritif. Emma looked at him disapprovingly but, with a toss of the head, he rejected the implied criticism. She continued to sip her champagne with obvious pleasure.

'You mean that Bragshaw was none other than the man who delivered the Chambertin to L'Esprit de Bourgogne restaurant?'

'Yes. But more than that. I spoke to Mrs Bragshaw immediately after you remembered the bizarre story of the van driver in Paris. Both were delivering wine, both dead in circumstances which looked self-inflicted, if not suicidal. Anyway, Mrs Bragshaw had told me that her husband had mentioned having "a bit of luck". Bragshaw had said nothing of this. I expect the money's hidden in his sock, because it certainly didn't reach his bank.'

'Well, he never got to enjoy it, did he?'

'Two van drivers. Both knew something. Both ended up dead. And how many more are there of whom we don't know? Anyway, I'm going to Paris to see the widow of the French van driver. It's about time I collected my car too!'

'It would be cheaper to abandon the car, wouldn't it? Parking fees and . . .'

He laughed. 'And then I'll see Lucien Lubeau. He's got some egg on his face.'

'Plonk on his parts is more like it,' she replied, looking at her Mickey Mouse watch. 'You'd better order. I've got to get to this party in Sloane Street. They say Lord Lucan is going to turn up.'

'And Ronald Biggs too, I suppose.'

'Barty.' She clasped her hands across the table and looked at him. 'That's two dead men we know about. Does it occur to you that, if someone knew about your enquiries, or thought you were getting anywhere, you just might be lined up as footings for a new French autoroute?'

'Rubbish. You're being dramatic, and anyway *nothing* will stop me getting the bastard behind all this. By the way, have you heard from your man in Liverpool?'

'No.'

'Well, why not ring him. See what the word is about that Chablis.'

'OK.' Her fashionable culottes were unflattering, he decided, as she went out of view, and if they didn't suit her, then whom did they suit?

She returned, her face triumphant. 'Our reporter managed to speak to somebody in Customs and Excise. The Chablis had come from France via Holland. But the thing is,' and here her eyes sparkled, 'the Customs and Excise *knew* before the ship arrived that the load was suspect — otherwise it would have gone through like other so-called Chablis which has come into the country.'

Fraser nodded. 'But where did the wine come from?'

'Probably Italian. Imported into France at a port called Sète. I've never heard of it.'

'I have. It's a major wine port near Marseille. Anyway, go on.'

'It seems the Italians have been dumping a lot of white wine in Sète.'

'And there,' continued Fraser, 'it becomes expensive and desirable Chablis by a stroke of the pen. It's the modern miracle. Not water into wine but plonk into profit.'

'Aren't you missing something?'

'Am I?' Bart's eyes narrowed.

She giggled. 'Barty! I do believe I'm one jump ahead of you. You remember? That article in the magazine about the American wine. McMac's, wasn't it? Didn't it say in the article that the wine might have come from Italy, although it was supposed to be French?'

'Emma, you're a genius. There was a time when I thought you had the brain of a tit and bum journalist but now I know differently. You're still a tit and bum journalist but with a rare added ingredient.'

'Do you know what I think?'

'No. Surprise me again, egg-head.'

'The French wine trade is throughly corrupt and complacent and at last their sins are being discovered.'

'If that's what you think, my little Emma—' he put his arm round her—'you're more of a scrambled egg-head.' He pulled her affectionately to his side as they walked into the London air in search of a cab. 'There's much more to it than that.'

# FRANCE

It was nice to be back behind the wheel. He enjoyed driving at any time and the sheer joy of belting down the A.6 autoroute was an added pleasure. Oblivious of the speed limit, he kept the needle hovering around 115 m.p.h., leaving Simcas and Citroëns floundering in his wake. Fraser's mind was as heated as the engine and turning over twice as fast.

Madame Dupont, widow of the French van driver, had agreed to see him when he called at her flat, high up in the drabness of Courbevoie. Young, attractive, still in mourning, though dressed in a dark red dungaree suit, she had seemed reserved at first when faced with the request for a discussion with an English solicitor. But when he told her of his desire to seek the truth of the '*affaire du Chameau Chambré*' she had let him in and, over a cup of coffee, had said all those things which she had wanted to say but had never said. No, of course her husband had never been a pervert. No, he had never kept magazines at home or in his van. Yes, he was happy in his job. No, he had no reason to commit suicide. No, he had never indulged in masochism. Yes, he might have agreed to the occasional spot of easy money.

At this point the conversation had gone rather quiet.

Fraser could sense that she was about to take the giant leap into the unknown. He had said nothing, waiting for her, letting her take her own time. The only noise had been the shrieks of children from the rest of the block playing on the balconies. The pause had given Fraser the chance to look around him, to take in the picture of the dead man, identical to the one used by the newspapers. The furnishings were new but utilitarian, purchased from a discount store near Senlis. From the kitchen came a slight hint of cooking smells. But overall, the memory which lingered as he accelerated past the Auxerre turning was of the pervading sadness, the air of a shrine, so reminiscent of his own recent past. It was as if the young girl were keeping the flat in a state of readiness for her husband's homecoming at supper-time. The silence had been broken as she walked to a teak wall cupboard. From a bottom corner she had produced a buff envelope, had handed it to him without a word. Inside, he had found 5,000 francs in new, 100-franc notes. They were held together by an elastic band, which also had a note scrawled upon it. It simply said, 'From a well-wisher.' Someone had pushed it through her door about two weeks previously. She hadn't known what to do about it, had told no one, was wondering what to do. No, she had no idea from where the money had come.

'But Francette? Who is she? What was she to my husband?' Her voice choked as she said the name.

'If I'm right,' he'd replied gently, 'there was no Francette. She never existed, was just part of a charade. Your husband was murdered. I can't prove it yet, so say nothing about our talk. And leave it to me.'

'Murdered? Claude murdered?'

'I think so.' He'd left shortly after, more convinced than ever that he was right. The money was a significant pointer.

The death of the van driver in isolation was not overtly

suspicious, but all the factors taken together led to the type of certainty of murder which was incapable of proof, the type of certainty which led to brick-planting and perjury.

The evening ahead with Lubeau would be interesting. More pride than wine would be swallowed. Lubeau had some words to eat. Better for his diet than Bœuf à la Mode.

## ATLANTIC CITY, NEW JERSEY

Senator Janus was not permitted to sit at the head of the boardroom table. Ostensibly in power of the company which owned McMac, nevertheless the power lay elsewhere — distinctly so. On looking at the five men sitting beside him, the Senator was uncomfortable, yet helpless. To the world he was their figurehead; to them, he was their captive, trapped by his own fondness for young boys approaching puberty. The price of their silence had been heavy but he had brought apparent respectability to a company involved in the liquor trade, a company anxious to make progress on Wall Street as a conglomerate called Great Pinewood Shores. The Senator, formerly a Secretary of State in a previous Republican administration, had been able to sweet-talk bankers, financiers, brokers, not only in Wall Street but also in Paris, where the shares of the company had been warmly regarded on the Bourse. He had done well and, so long as the group was prospering, he was secure. But now the present crisis had changed everything.

'These goddamned Frenchies are sure as hell scaring the shit out of me.' The speaker was Louis Spiggola, who owned the controlling interest in the corporation, and if Spiggola were concerned, then those around him were sure to follow. Not a man to scare easily and never a man to be physically afraid, everyone knew that his fear was born only of the unknown. 'Anyone any idea what the hell's going on?' he concluded.

No one said anything but there were a few grunts and shakes of denial.

'Goddamn it, what the hell do I pay you guys for?' He pointed a dark brown, stubby finger at each in turn. 'I'll tell you why I pay you. It's to get off your goddamned asses.' The jet black hair was heavily brilliantined, so that it never moved, despite the vigorous shaking of the head. Again there was a silence but this time someone felt constrained to break it.

'Our legal people are working on it. They're filing a lawsuit against the suppliers.' There was a nasal whine to the voice.

'We're sure all the stuff is from Italy, are we? Like, I mean all three million bottles?'

'Sure we're sure. And we're gonna make life pretty uncomfortable. Or so the lawyers say. And they don't come no smarter than our lawyers.'

Spiggola thought for a moment. 'Crap! Lawyers ain't gonna sort this out in time. Time we ain't got.' He turned to Danny O'Grady, who was the company's financial adviser in New York. 'What's the latest in our shares?'

'The Dow Jones is up but our shares are down under $2.30. That's $6.80 altogether since the trouble broke.'

'See what I mean?' The boss glared round the table. 'Time we ain't got. If our price keeps falling like that then someone's gonna take *us* over, someone who reckons things are gonna change and that all our assets ain't bad.'

'Kinda ironic, ain't it? Us being in line for a takeover.'

No one felt inclined to laugh. The irony was too bitter.

'Know what I'm thinking?' It was Spiggola again. 'I'm thinking we should never have gotten ourselves involved in buying that French vineyard. Sure, it seemed a good idea at the time. But now Wall Street turns a sneeze in Beaune into 'flu in New York.'

Senator Janus decided to join in. 'And I guess that not one of our bottles from our own vineyard in Bordeaux is suspect?'

'You're right there, Senator. Not one. Our business in France is A.I. legit!'

'If it's any consolation,' said O'Grady, 'the shares of every major liquor corporation with European assets are taking a hammering.'

'One man's loss is another man's gain.' Spiggola frowned. 'And, if we don't get this thing sorted out pretty damn quick, then there's gonna be some new faces sittin' round this table.'

'Any more news on that Kressin fella, killed down in Dallas?' someone asked.

'Nope.' Spiggola was positive. 'Not regarded as relevant to anything with which we're concerned. But keep thinkin'. Anythin' else in the air?' For a moment he thought there would be no response but then the man at the foot of the table, who had not spoken, nodded his head. His name was Rudi Ramalpo, the most dangerous person present. As far as Janus could understand, his job was to listen, seek out and then exterminate. It was a job at which he was particularly accomplished. 'Can't say anything for certain yet, Louis, but there was a guy shot in New York. If I'd had another two days, I could have told you for certain.'

'Told us what?' The intervention was forceful, as the listener seized anxiously on anything which had a tinge of optimism.

'That maybe this guy who was shot was the same guy who complained about wine he'd bought in Chicago and New Orleans. And maybe elsewhere, for all I know.'

'Hey! Wouldn't that just be something!' Spiggola lit a cigar and nodded his head. The aquiline features smiled wolfishly. 'But where does it get us?'

'Nowhere, unless someone knows who it was. We find the guy that fired the shots. Then we find out why he fired them or who paid him to fire them. Then maybe we're somewhere.'

'What about the cops?'

'They ain't got nothin' on it. Just a muggin'—just a statistic.'

'OK. We'll adjourn. But when we come back here, sure as hell I want facts, facts and a rising price on Wall Street. Ain't nothin' else will do.'


# BEAUNE

'You must think me a poor judge of the state of the French wine business,' said Lucien Lubeau as he surveyed his plate of *escargots*.

'Right in one. But why were you wrong?' Fraser looked at the snails with disdain. 'I don't know what you see in those things. Little lumps of rubber.'

'Ah. We eat them, not for the snails, but for the garlic butter,' the Frenchman replied. By now his white napkin was tucked into the top of his pullover, his eyes rolling in anticipation. An *ingénu* would have said that the man hadn't eaten for weeks. In fact his lunch, down the road at Fixin, had finished only three hours before.

'So what's the gossip?'

'That someone very clever is manipulating a situation. There was a meeting among the leading négociants, but even I don't know what was decided. They say it was a shambles but I doubt it. There have been top line discussions in Paris.'

'Come on,' chided Fraser. 'You're telling me nothing. Nothing I can't read in *Newsweek* or *L'Express*.'

'You should be looking for someone who knows the French wine business through and through. Someone who knows the ways in which the unscrupulous can pass off Italy's contribution to the great wine lake as Chablis or Bourgogne. It can be done.' There was a Gallic shrug. 'Such a person is the great manipulator.'

'Here in Beaune?'

'Possible, but I think not. We've spoken before of the Fraud Squad. For what was attempted in the States or Liverpool you look at Sète, or Marseille, or Holland. And of course certain English companies have been convicted in the past.' A wave of the arms accompanied a further Gallic shrug. 'Exposure is inevitable.'

'But the tip-off in Liverpool? That's what interests me.'

'Curious. I'm convinced that you're looking for someone out to discredit not just the city of Beaune or a particular négociant, or a particular grower, or of course your client.'

'Someone out to discredit the whole of the French wine industry?'

For a moment Lubeau picked at his teeth, much to Fraser's disgust. The two men were weighing up the implications. Then: 'Perhaps.'

'Someone who *knows* the French wine industry, yet has no love for it,' prompted Fraser.

'And someone who stands to gain from its discomfort.' The heat in the small restaurant and the richness of the food caused Lubeau to mop his brow with the already much used napkin.

'Right. That's the mass market. But then there's the Chambertin in London, the Volnay in Paris, the Château Plaisance 1966 in New Orleans and so on.'

'Orchestration?' mused Lubeau.

'Someone pulling lots of strings?'

Lubeau shook his head. '*Non*. I meant someone creating a crescendo.'

'Someone from America perhaps?'

The Frenchman said nothing. He raised the ballon, swirled the glass, angled it, sniffed appreciatively and at last tasted the Fixin '76. He nodded knowingly. 'Recommended to me at lunch-time today. And the grower was right. California. That would have a certain logic.'

'Let me think aloud. French wines are expensive; many would say overpriced. If someone can produce a reasonably comparable product at a competitive price, then a vast market opens up. Agreed?'

'Yes.' Lubeau's jowls filled like sails in the wind.

Fraser continued. 'The Californian wine industry, while a relative novice, has a more scientific approach to wine production, coupled with a better climate, so that they have become a real threat to French domination of traditional markets.'

Lubeau waved his forearm perilously close to Fraser's face. 'No. I don't agree with that. First because the Californians do not yet produce enough. Secondly because they do not have the *cachet* which still attaches to the name of Lafite, Louis Latour or Bouchard.'

'All right. But if those names were discredited . . . ?' Fraser left the rhetoric in the air deliberately. 'If a picture is painted of a crooked French wine industry, with random examples of the greatest names being questioned, as well as the mass market?'

'You have my interest. You mean that you get the world believing they can no longer trust the integrity of the French label. You offer them a product with an unquestioned, untarnished pedigree. At a better price.'

Fraser nodded and continued. 'And you proceed to increase your share of the bulk and the quality market. Eliminate any lingering snob appeal enjoyed by the French.'

'It's possible.'

'Assume I'm right. It may not be California. It could be Chile, South Africa or even Australia, although I would regard them all as long shots and ill-equipped to expand their market share. The Californians are already well established in Europe. Now is the ideal time to make their push. So, assume we're talking of Californians discrediting the French market, who would I be looking for?'

'Again I would say someone who knows the French wine industry. And there are many of them. American companies have bought into France. French growers have left here to set up their vineyards in California. Even the great Rothschild himself has seen the value of investment in California.'

'Agreed. But then we eliminate all those who still have investment in France. Otherwise their left hand is simply biting their right.'

'Then you look for a Californian company which is well placed in Europe and ready to increase its market share. Sales of our wines are falling and our competitors, like the Californians, could be the winners.'

'And the auctions? What about them?'

'The prices have fallen. First Growth prices fell a remarkable twenty-five per cent.'

'If a Californian company could increase its share of the market, of the World market, by say three per cent, that would be big money, wouldn't it?'

'Too much for one company from California to achieve. But all the Californian wine industry could gain much more than that and the best placed companies would gain most. Millions of dollars a year.'

'And what next? More revelations in Beaune? More tales of corruption here?'

'I don't know. My confidence has all gone.'

# BEAUNE

The previous evening had ended on a note of some hilarity as he had shaken hands with Lubeau.

'My doctor would not be pleased with me,' the Frenchman had said.

'Why not?'

'Because I'm on a diet. My doctor has restricted me to one meal and one woman per day.'

'Then why so sad? At least you've still got a woman to look forward to.'

'Alas, no! After lunch I stopped off at a friend's!'

'If you don't like the diet, then change the doctor.' Fraser's jocular advice had gone down well and the men had parted laughing, with a promise from Lubeau to phone.

The telephone by Fraser's bed rang. 'Hello?'

It was Lubeau. '*Bonjour. Bien dormi?*'

'I'm fine. And how's your diet today?'

'Excellent! Today my doctor will be less angry. Today I shall have no food and two women. Do you think he will approve?'

'At least you'll die with a smile on your face. Anyway, what's new?' Fraser twisted round on the bed, so that his bad leg stuck out in front of him like a gadget on a pen-knife.

'We were talking of auctions. There's a major American auction taking place in New Orleans. No, it's not Christie's. It's a new American company moving into the auction market, called Muir Hawthorne. It's their first auction. A while back, a representative came to here and Bordeaux. He was searching out, as a special favour, several cases of the very best wines for inclusion. This was,

of course, long before these *little difficulties* arose. I think
you'll find that many of the most famous names have
cooperated. If what he said was correct, then the auction
was to include Châteaux Petrus, Lafite, Cheval Blanc
and many others.'

'The price of Château Petrus was reaching absurdly
high prices anyway, before all this panic. I seem to recall
an auction in Chicago, held by Christie's?'

'That's right. This auction will test what's happening to
the market in America.'

'So, one should wait for the auction? See if the prices
steady?'

'Maybe. But I was thinking somewhat differently. I've
been asking some questions. It's just possible we were on
the right lines last night. There's an indefinable buzz
going round. Perhaps it's just my desire to have the good
name of the French wine industry cleared. Don't
laugh—I believe it *does* have a good name. This set me
thinking about the container load of the best that France
can produce. It was here, in Beaune, yesterday, being
loaded. I've just checked that. This morning it should be
arriving at the stuffing depot in Bordeaux.'

'Stuffing depot?' said Fraser, struggling with the
meaning of the word.

'Yes. It's the place where the growers deliver their wines
when their own load is insufficient to fill an entire
container. So the truck which left here yesterday will be
partially full. The remainder of the space will be taken up
with the wines from Bordeaux, the Loire and
Champagne. When the container is full, the load will
move to the Bordeaux docks where the container will be
loaded on a ship for Savannah.'

'Savannah? Why Savannah? That's in Georgia, isn't it?'

'Because that's where Muir Hawthorne have their
headquarters and their cellars. Christie's have their
auctions in Chicago, or New Orleans, or elsewhere, but

keep the wines in their New York cellars. There's no point in the wine following the auctioneer round the country. It saves expense and protects the wine, which was a concept almost unknown in the States.'

'So what are you telling me, then?'

'That Muir Hawthorne, at least, have known the contents of that container for weeks. If someone is out to discredit the French market, then they've had ample time to prepare a duplicate set of bottles, ready to be switched.'

Fraser thought about it for a moment. It would fit the picture, be the ultimate scandal to have the best known, most influential and prestigious wine buyers duped at auction, for they would buy the wine on its name and description in the catalogue without tasting. 'Bordeaux is a long way from here.'

'There's a flight from Dijon at ten thirty. If you want to take it, then start driving to the airport now. I'll have a reservation made for you. And a car at the other end if you wish?'

'OK. But I don't know what I'll do.'

'Keep an eye on that truck. From the moment it leaves the stuffing depot. That's the buzz.'

'Sounds like speculation to me.'


# BORDEAUX

As he sat in the Islander, 6,000 feet above South-West France, Fraser considered Lubeau's tip. It sounded a long shot, but then Lubeau's mistress was well placed. If she were right, then the tampering had to be done in France or the USA. On the boat would be impossible.

Having acted for a client who had made money from container-leasing, Fraser knew that anyone determined to break in could do so, either through the flimsiness of the roof or through the doors themselves. All that was required was a supply of Customs rivets and a batch of seals, all of which were readily available in the black market world of transport cafés.'

Of course a switch of wines could have happened between Beaune and Bordeaux, but this was unlikely, he decided, because the greatest wines for investment were the clarets to be loaded round Bordeaux.

Everything depended on Lubeau, or rather his mistress, for one of them certainly had a crafty ear close to the ground and, judging by the slight licking of the lips and rolling of the eyes, Fraser judged that Lubeau had indeed been dependent upon his mistress for information. As she was secretary to one of the biggest négociants in Beaune she was in the know. But what he would do if he saw anything suspicious was unresolved. The pilot tapped him on the shoulder, showing him that the airport was now in sight and, moments later, he found himself on the tarmac, overnight bag in hand, and a hungry feeling in his stomach. There was no great hurry for, if Lucien were right, the container wouldn't finish loading until 6.00 p.m.

After a leisurely lunch he picked up the hired Renault and joined the N.89, knowing that he was looking for a dark blue truck with a white container and a Burgundy registration. Lucien Lubeau had been well informed, for just before 6.30 he saw the truck heading for Bordeaux. He followed it into the outskirts, where it was evident that the driver was not heading for the docks. A couple of lefts and a right from the main road and Fraser watched the truck enter a yard in a broken-down back street. Nothing sinister in that, except for the brief glimpse of a seemingly identical container truck already standing in the same yard. Fraser cruised slowly past in his Renault 5, while someone unseen shut the gates, isolating the yard from the curious.

The surrounding area was more desolate than derelict, gaps between the houses appearing like pipe-smokers' teeth, the remaining houses on the street being mainly empty, the residents gone to modern blocks in other parts of the city. A bomb had probably flattened a line of houses nearly forty years before and the yard had been created from the rubble.

Fraser parked in a side street not quite opposite, where the Renault was anonymous in a line of cars outside houses yet to be cleared of occupants. It was still daylight, but darkening, and from where he sat Fraser could see the corrugated iron gates and fencing which surrounded the two trucks and their loads. One thing was certain: whatever happened on the other side of the gates would be unseen. He was about to seek a better vantage-point when the gate opened and two men appeared, both dressed in dungaree suits and each carrying what appeared to be an overnight bag. They went out of Fraser's sight but he was able to catch up enough to see them enter a corner café, about 150 yards away. Looking fairly inconspicuous himself in a blue denim jacket and trousers, he followed their route, noticing only the occasional sound of voices from the gaunt, broken-down façades of the once-fine properties.

The café proved to be a cosy Routier and the two men sitting inside, each now with a glass, were studying some papers. Uncertain as to what to do, he hovered outside, conscious that the weather had changed and that a chilling Atlantic wind was doing him no good at all. The prospect of checking in at the best hotel was tempting, particularly as the *patron* was setting up the cutlery for the two men, who plainly were going to eat. Resignedly he cowered into a doorway to keep vigil.

So engrossed was he that, in turn, he failed to notice a

Citroën Pallas pass the cafe for a second time in as many minutes. It was over an hour before the men paid the bill and reappeared, walking briskly back to the yard. Fraser had taken a few paces when the Citroën illuminated the backs of the two men and then a clang of the gates and bolts heralded impossibility of access. Less afraid than he'd expected, Fraser studied the derelict building beside the yard, its front door half open, just as the last owner or vagrant had left it. Reluctantly he went in and was welcomed by a scuttle of movement and a stench of time gone by, each of which created its own potent barrier of fear.

Unwilling to take another step without assessing the position, he flicked his lighter and the extremities of the hallway danced before him. To his left was a steep staircase, with an iron balustrade which spiralled upwards for three floors. The once-white walls were pock-marked, crumbling and rotted with damp. The floor was littered with the dust of time, with rubble, broken glass and chunks of plaster. But the stairs looked solid enough. A rat tumbled over the banister and disappeared from sight. Steeling himself and moving as silently as he could, the light still flickering in his hand, he started his ascent. Silence was impossible but he felt no more noisy than the rats, the broken glass, the polythene, than the noise of tumbledown dereliction.

Concentrating on every step forward and up, Fraser failed to notice a movement behind him just outside the house, failed to notice someone pause at the half-open door; failed to notice a shadowy figure enter the hallway which he had left only seconds before.

On the landing were three doors, one of which led to the rear of the building. Less cautious now of the need for silence, but aware that any light would show, he extinguished the lighter, hoping to recall the instant geography for long enough to make progress. Keeping his right hand trailing along the wall, he found that he was now on lino, walking silently, the broken plaster having disappeared. It was as if someone had cleaned the room. Home for a tramp perhaps? As a thought it was unattractive.

At the glassless window he found that one shutter had long ago fallen and the other was partially open. Gingerly at first, then with more confidence, he peered out. There, about six feet below him and twenty feet away, were the trucks. The drivers had disconnected the trailers and each tractor unit was now manœuvring, switching position to line up to join the other's load. From his vantage-point it was like watching the mating dance of a pair of giant scorpions, until there was post-coital silence as the engines were switched off.

What now? Switch the container numbers? Maybe not if they'd matched the numbers in advance, which they could have done, knowing the precise details of the load for Savannah. They'd had days, weeks even, in which to obtain bottles, corks, labels, wooden cases, cardboard cartons and documentation to make up a duplicate load of cheap wine in expensive bottles, ready for the switch. With the time available, preparation of a duplicate container, identical in appearance and identical in number was simple. Although Fraser knew that central computers tracked the location of every container, by reference to its registered number, there was nothing to prevent the unscrupulous from having two containers with identical numbers, to be used to their convenience and advantage.

Corks, labels, cases and boxes were easy to come by in Dijon and Bordeaux. All that remained was for the number plates on the trailers to be switched and this was precisely what the two men were doing at this very moment. In just a few minutes the invaluable load destined for Savannah had been stolen.

Whether it was the creaking of a floorboard or a sense of movement in the room Fraser wasn't sure, but something caused him to start, to draw back from the window. He looked over his shoulder and saw, some four paces away in the gloom, the unmistakable figure of a man of no great height carrying the advantage of a pointed revolver. The man's face was invisible and the figure, swathed in black, merged completely into the background.

The voice which spoke was forceful, very Gallic and slightly guttural. 'Hands up.' Fraser would have understood the French, even without the added motioning of the weapon. He did as ordered, turning inwards from the window. It was scarcely a situation for which he was suited. A degree in Law and a hopalong leg made him an unlikely candidate for acts of flamboyant heroism. But he was surprised at how calm he felt in his helplessness, his brain working full bore, his eyes searching the darkness, trying to get their measure of the intruder.

'Who are you? What are you doing?' A movement of the gun accompanied the words, stressing the importance of a quick answer. But the questions were not easily answered, for who was the assailant? A look-out man for the men down below? A mastermind of the fraud, or what?

The answer, when it came, was spoken slowly and with precision. 'I'm English and am investigating a shipment of wine to the USA.'

The reply seemed to satisfy the stranger—at least in part. 'Your name, then?'

'Fraser. Bartholomew Fraser.' It sounded incongruous in the surroundings.

A semblance of movement suggested that the man was nodding his head. The response, spoken quietly, contained respect. 'Ah! Monsieur Bartholomew. I've heard of you.' The gun was lowered. 'I too am being paid to watch this wine, as I will explain later. What's happening?'

'First, tell me who *you* are.'

'Later. But we have a similar interest. Of that I assure you.' As he spoke, the man came forward and the solicitor could see a slim figure, standing five feet seven, with a thinnish face and dark hair. He was aged perhaps twenty-eight but with a face which commanded the authority of a man twice as old. As the Frenchman squeezed into position by the window, Fraser smelt a delicate touch of eau de Cologne, mixed with the familiar aroma of French tobacco. 'Have they swapped the containers?' The Frenchman spoke with the confidence of someone who was expecting a positive answer.

Fraser whispered confirmation. 'I would think they've almost finished.'

As if the men below had heard the whispered conversation, they could be seen nodding to each other before moving out of sight. There was the sound of scraping metal as the yard gates were opened and then slammed shut.

'Chambon. Henri Chambon — that's my name. I'm an agent, being paid by a syndicate to keep an eye on this wine. You were mentioned in *Le Figaro* the other day as looking after the interests of Monsieur le Breton. Furthermore, you've been making some enquiries in Beaune. Am I right?'

'Yes.'

'Then our interests are indeed identical and what you saw simply confirmed what I anticipated. I came prepared for just this eventuality and I have a plan. With your help, it will be easier.'

Fraser's voice was throaty and dry. 'I might be able to help you.'

'Good. Then I'll explain.'

'Where are you?' enquired Henri Chambon from his bedside telephone at the Terminus Hotel, Bordeaux.

'Would you believe I followed that wretched truck all the way to Sète?'

'Why not? Not in the least surprised. It's the major port for receiving wine from Greece, Italy and Algeria. In Sète, at the wave of a wand or, more usually, with the help of a label and some glue, they perform the modern miracle: not water into wine, but worthless plonk into priceless Petrus! Anyway, what did the driver do?' Chambon had a very good idea of the answer.

'Just as you said. He dropped off the container at a small warehouse near the Quai des Moulins. It's a depository for wine importers. Their name is Florentine et Cie.'

'Excellent! So now we know the French centre of operations. The plonk arrives here in bulk from Italy, I expect. If I'm right, in that warehouse they bottle the plonk using identical bottles, identical corks and suitable labels to match the best wines of France. All they need are a few good contacts in the vineyards and a little forewarning.'

Fraser agreed. 'With the type of money at stake, a few francs can buy invaluable information.'

'Examples are all too frequent, my friend.'

'So what now? Bring in the Fraud Squad to do a raid on this warehouse?'

'No. Not for two reasons. First, you and me are the only people who know the present position. I want it kept that way. Bringing in the Fraud Squad could give rise to all sorts of leaks of information. I'm not even telling my principals. Even among them, there could be a Judas. Secondly, jumping too soon could mean catching the French minnows and letting escape the real sharks, who lurk in much deeper water. Bart, my friend, we sit tight. We've done well, for the truck which I watched delivered its container which was then loaded. The next time we see it will be in Savannah.'

'And now?'

'I'll fly to Montpellier in the morning. Meet me at the airport. Tomorrow night we'll have a look round Florentine's warehouse.'

Next day, their plan thoroughly mastered during an afternoon visit to the warehouse, the two men waited under cover of darkness, invisible in the shadows opposite the building's silhouetted exterior.

Their earlier visit had proved that access was difficult, yet not impossible. The building stood in its own compound, guarded by a wire mesh fence of recent origin. Scaling it was out of the question and the only entrance was through a pair of double gates, which were kept locked even in daylight. Their mechanism was operated from somewhere in the office at the front corner of the warehouse.

'Shall we go, then?' enquired Chambon.

Silently they crossed the small estate road and down a track, which ran along the rear boundary of the property. Although the fence was new, Chambon's wire-cutters made an opening without difficulty and within seconds they were standing in the yard, the back of the building about ten paces away, the night watchman some eighty yards away in his post at the front. Dragging his left leg behind him, Fraser kept pace with the Frenchman, stride for stride, clinging close to the shadows of the wall all the while.

They rounded the corner at the front of the building

and saw the light from the night watchman's window. Ducking beneath it, they reached the door which provided the only possible access, for the vehicular entrance was securely barred and bolted. Above the office door was a porch and, with a hand from Fraser, the Frenchman climbed upon it, knowing that just inside was the guard, with his flask of coffee and a cheap novel.

The small, opaque glass window set into the door was perfect for the operation. From just above the window, Fraser suspended a nut and bolt on a piece of string, fixed with a large glob of chewing-gum. Another length of string, much longer than the first, led down from Chambon's hand to the weight. Satisfied with the result, Fraser signalled to Chambon and disappeared from sight around the corner of the warehouse.

A moment or two passed and then came the expected noise: a knocking, or rather just an isolated tap. Seconds later the noise came again as Chambon pulled his length of string so that the nut and bolt tapped on the window. It wasn't blatant. On the contrary, it was an insidious noise, designed to arouse the curiosity rather than the fear of the man on the other side of the door. Gradually Chambon accelerated the regularity of the tapping of metal on glass until Fraser wondered whether the man within must not be deaf for having taken no step to investigate. The idea had been Fraser's, learnt from a childhood game, and had been applauded by Chambon when both men realized that to knock at the door in a secure compound was the last way to get it opened, especially at nearly midnight.

Fraser drew back as a sliver of light appeared. Then the door opened, bathing the area in light. As he caught sight of the watchman, Fraser could almost see the man's mind working as he stood puzzling out the infuriating tapping noise. At last he saw the string leading to the porch and Fraser could see the man's eyes following the line of the string as he took a half-step forward to investigate its source.

At that moment Chambon jumped on to the man's back, grabbing him round the neck in a furious grip.

'*Merde*!' exclaimed the guard, as he was knocked to the ground by the force of the impact from behind. Fraser too moved fast, and while Chambon pinned down the man, Fraser forced a handkerchief into his mouth before they dragged the victim into his office and shut the door.

The night watchman was well into his sixties, somewhat frail and not minded to be troublesome when faced with two men in stocking masks. Even Fraser had been frightened by his own appearance when he had glanced at himself in the mirror earlier in the day. The squat ugliness of the distortion was terrifying, and he felt pangs of sympathy for the man, who probably knew nothing of the illegalities which the warehouse appeared to house. But there was little time for sympathy as they busily tied the man's arms and legs from behind, so that the frail body was arched back like a bow and unable to move.

Satisfied that the man was helpless, they left him and went into the next office, with its cheap desk and rows of invoices hanging from bulldog clips on a wall. On the desk was a telephone and, beside it, lay a personal directory of phone numbers. Fraser was about to pocket it.

'No, we don't want anyone to know what we've found. Just copy down any numbers which look useful, which might be worth following up. I'll have a look through these invoices.'

The job was not quickly done, for the book contained at least thirty numbers and when in doubt Fraser copied out the number, rather than risk losing the information for ever.

'Finished?' enquired Chambon.

'Yes.'

'Interesting?'

'Maybe. Though some of these numbers don't have names beside them. They're the interesting ones. And you?'

'No. The invoices all look legitimate. You'd need an accountant here, totting up all the arrivals of wine, all the sales to see if the figures balance. And I bet they don't.'

Fraser nodded in agreement. 'Let's look round the rest of the place, then.' As he spoke Fraser opened another door, which led from the office into the main part of the warehouse. At night the interior was lit only by a single floodlight, some forty feet above the ground, which filled the room with stark contrasts of light and shade. Opposite them and all the way down the hall was wine: wine in boxes, wine in bottles, wine in plastic containers and wine in giant tonneaux. It was an impressive sight and, as they stood in the central gangway, they could see to the far end of the premises where there were rows of bottling plants, complete with lines of bottles ready to be filled.

'Nothing unusual so far,' said Chambon as they walked slowly down the warehouse, looking at labels, seeking out the wine brought back by the truck from Bordeaux. There was no sign of it. 'What would you have done with it? Would you have sold it?'

Fraser thought for a moment. 'No. It's no time to be selling this quantity of wine. But there's no container in here, so it must have been unloaded. The wine might have been taken away during the day or it might have been re-labelled. But I don't see any point in that. Put yourself in *their* position. On its way to Savannah is plonk in disguise. In its place, Florentine's have the finest wines that France can produce but, with a falling market, it doesn't make sense to sell them. In fact it only makes sense at all if it's part of a major plan to discredit the French wine industry. Otherwise all they've done is steal

something which, however good, is being discredited.'
The whispered conversation took place as the men walked
past the bottling plant and started to retrace their steps
down the other side of the warehouse.

In the distance were the two offices but, before that,
were stacked giant crates, standing all of ten feet high, all
the way down the building. 'Give me a leg up again,' said
Chambon and the next morning he was standing on one
of the wooden crates. 'This is it,' he exclaimed sharply as
he surveyed a hoard of wine in cases, boxes, and cartons,
all bearing the names of the great vineyards of France.
Behind the protection of the crates was the secret of the
warehouse.

'I don't think I can get up there,' said Fraser. But even
as he spoke, he was pushing at the corner of a crate. To
his surprise it moved easily. It was empty and, with a grin
at Chambon, which went unappreciated behind the
stocking mask, the Englishman was first into the secret
area.

There were giant drums containing corks ready for
use; corks either stolen from famous vineyards or
manufactured on the black market to help in the passing
off. On a table lay neat stacks of labels in boxes to
complete the charade.

While Fraser studied the damning evidence, Chambon
was padding about among the cases, taking photographs.
'*Ici*,' he called and Fraser went over. There, carefully
stacked, were the cases of wine recently returned from
Bordeaux.

They started to check the items against their list, when
a noise from the entrance to the warehouse caused them
both to freeze. Someone had come into the building.
There was the sound of movement, of a door opening and
closing and the echoing exclamation of surprise as the
new arrival saw the night watchman bound and gagged
on the floor. And there was only one way out of the

warehouse. A wave of nausea gripped Fraser as the depth of the predicament struck home, for they were cornered and barely concealed from any search-party.

'What do we do?' Fraser found his voice croaky and unreliable.

'Nothing. We sit tight. Maybe they won't search. And they certainly won't call the police. That's the last thing they want.'

'But they're bound to come. The night watchman knows that we're still in here.'

'Do what I say. I don't know what it'll be but whatever it is, you do it without question. OK?'

Silent now, they crouched behind a pallet stacked with wine cases and they waited, hoping to hear the noise of departure but expecting the worst. And the worst happened. There was a resonance around the warehouse as the night watchman and at least one other person left the light of the office for the shadows of the warehouse and Fraser knew that discovery of their hiding-place was a certainty. The crate pushed to one side, giving access to the sensitive part of the building, was a give-away which no one could ignore and which was bound to be investigated.

He shivered, recalling the violent death of Claude Dupont in Paris, of the death of Arthur Bragshaw under a tube train in London. He was meddling in the affairs of killers and his own death seemed predictably imminent. Footsteps coming down the central aisle came closer until they paused just a crate's width away from Fraser's hiding-place. Again he could sense the decision being taken by the searchers. They had seen the pushed-aside crate and could guess that their quarry was close at hand.

His heart pumping wildly, his eyes bulging with fear, Fraser crouched uncomfortably, awaiting execution. The footsteps moved again as the men entered the gap between the crates. Ashamed at the way he was trembling, Fraser drew some comfort from Chambon tucked in beside him, gun in hand. Six feet, five feet, four feet. The searchers came into view, one with arm outstretched, also armed, ready to fire at the slightest movement.

Fraser could not believe that Chambon would be frozen by fear, yet here they were, crouched and cowering, with a killer split seconds away from seeing them. It was then that a shot rang out, exploding deafeningly around the building and the room went black. Fraser convinced himself that he was dead, so sudden was the transformation, yet he had felt no pain.

'Run, run,' called Chambon. Uncertain what had happened, Fraser rose to do so just as Chambon sprang at the man with the gun, knocking him off balance. The agent's aim had been true and the shot had extinguished the solitary spotlight. 'Run, run,' he encouraged Fraser, who leapt in the direction of the night watchman, knowing that he occupied the gap which was needed. For the second time that evening, the man was unlucky as Fraser caught him sideways, sending him flying back into the corner of a packing case. Dazed and frightened, he was happy to lie where he fell.

As Fraser ran, he was conscious of the noise of scuffling behind him. Another shot rang out and somewhere unseen a bullet ricocheted from a wall into the blackness above. Dragging his leg behind him, nevertheless he reached the office unharmed. Only then did he stop, turn and look back in the direction of the fighting and found that his legs had gone into liquidation, useless, trembling and full of fear. There was a shout of pain, followed by a deafening roar as a stack of cases tumbled to the ground. Then there was silence. Alone now with his beating heart and numbed brain Fraser stood baffled. He tried to steel himself to go back, to find out, maybe to assist, but he couldn't do it. The clasp of terror was overpowering as he leant against a wall, peering at the unseen depths.

He waited panting, uncertain and ashamed of his cowardice until a hint of movement reached his ears. 'Bar-tee!' It was the agent's voice, soft and enquiring. But Fraser's petrified tongue could manage no more than a croak of recognition. Chambon's figure filled the doorway, his face smiling, his hair tousled, his pullover torn and a reddening stain of blood already apparent on his sleeve.

'Quick, quick!' Chambon nodded towards the yard and, as he turned, he bolted the door from the office to the warehouse, leaving the night watchman and his companion locked in the chill silence of the black interior.

'Well done,' said Chambon as Fraser drove the car without undue haste or noise, for Chambon's arm prevented him from driving. 'You did well.'

But Fraser knew differently. He said nothing.

Back in the Grand Hotel, Fraser called the number of a doctor known to Chambon. The wound was not serious, merely superficial, but it required some skilled attention to prevent infection and, as they waited for the doctor to arrive, it was Fraser who spoke. 'So what have we got?'

'Florentine's are a front for someone much bigger and, as that bastard with the gun was American, my guess is that's where we'll find the epicentre.'

Fraser thought back to his conversation with Lubeau, when they had bounced off the wall the idea that the Californians had a vested interest in discrediting the French. 'You're sure he was American?'

'Positive,' laughed Chambon. 'A knee in his balls produced some real Brooklyn language.' As he lay back on the bed, Chambon pulled a towel firmly over the wound but, even so, managed a swig from a bottle of Armagnac. 'What about those phone numbers?'

Fraser produced his notes. 'Quite a few of them are in America. They're the ones without names beside them.'

'How do you know?'

'They've all got the code for direct dial to the States.'

'Ring the American numbers. Any pretext will do.'

Fraser went to the phone and for the next twenty minutes worked steadily through the list, each number proving to be that of a hotel. 'There's only two more to go,' said Fraser. 'So far we've got Los Angeles, Hawaii, Atlanta and Washington. Not a clue as to the identity of the person at the other end.' He dialled again. There was silence for a  moment, broken only by Chambon wincing slightly as he moved to a more comfortable position. 'And you can add the Hyatt Regency at Savannah to the list now.'

'Savannah! There's a link anyway. All we need to know is who was staying at the hotel in Savannah and we've got it.'

'Well, I guess the Hyatt at Savannah might have had more than the occasional guest in the last few months.' Fraser felt drained, physically and mentally.

'I don't think the auctioneers are involved, though.' Chambon was thinking aloud.

'I think they're being used.'

'The final *coup de grâce* for the reputation of the French wine industry.'

'Unless we expose the truth now.'

'No. Not yet. We've got to identify the mastermind and the evidence has got to be strong—particularly if we're dealing with America now.'

'You mean the influence of organized crime there?'

'Sure. If you can't buy the first judge, then you pay more for the judges in the Appeal Court. You frame the prosecutor. You blackmail the witnesses. You'll have heard the stories as well.'

Fraser nodded. 'So we just have to let it ride.'

'Agreed. If my plan works, then we'll smoke out these bastards in America anyway.'

Fraser was about to reply when there was a knock at the door. It was the doctor.


# NEW ORLEANS


Bartholomew Fraser eased back the angle of his reclining chair. In front of him, the swimming pool glistened as he dried off in the heat of the southern sun, eighteen floors up above the sprawl of the city. Lying next to him, her figure amply displayed in brief black bikini, lay Emma, her eyes closed in bliss. With the temperature rising and the sight of Emma's slender limbs and generous breasts so close at hand, he felt threatened by a severe case of overheating.

'The auction's in an hour.'

'Must we go?' Emma's voice was reluctant.

'Well, I must and I don't think your Editor will approve your expenses chit unless you come up with something pretty good. If you remember — that's what you're here for.'

'I hadn't forgotten. But I can do what everyone else does. Rely on informants and my vivid imagination. *You* go to the auction and tell me what happens. I'll paint in the human side afterwards.' She twisted on to one elbow, so that her sun-tanned face added power to the plea. 'I'm much happier sitting here.'

'Aren't we all?' He tapped her on the nose. 'I'm ashamed of you, Emma. You can't expect me, a solicitor, to participate in that type of charade.' His tone was mocking.

'Pompous old fool. Even stripped to the waist, you still look like a stuffed shirt.' She ran her finger gently along her mouth and trailed her other hand along his thigh. 'Not even if . . .'

'No. Not even if.' His interruption was quick. It had to be, for the sight of her was almost irresistible. She poured two glasses of champagne and kissed him on the cheek as she passed the glass over. 'Come on, Barty. Henri's already at the auction. He doesn't need us.'

'Henri! If I'm not there, he'll shoot me.'

'OK. Just ten minutes more in the sun, then.' She stretched herself luxuriously, finished her champagne and poured another glass. 'It's a shame to go into a stuffy old hall with a lot of stuffy old wine-lovers, that's all.'

Fraser stretched out a hand and stroked her hair, his thoughts of the good fortune that the Editor had agreed to contribute to her expenses if she provided some copy from New Orleans. No copy, no money, had been the deal, and since her arrival Emma had shown no desire to file the briefest of stories for publication.

'Barty?'

'Yes.'

'You'd better tell me what it's all about. I mean, what is going to happen today.'

'You really want to know?' On seeing her nod her head, he continued. 'Down in the auction room, it'll be packed. There'll be wine buffs, amateurs, experts, speculators, investors, restaurateurs, journalists, Japanese, Americans, British, and even the French. They'll be watching each other, watching the way in which the prices are reacting.' It had been four weeks since his visit to the warehouse in Sète and the identity of the American connection was still a mystery, and both he and Chambon pinned great faith on the auction.

'What do you think'll happen?'

'God knows! The whole of the European market is in ferment. It's not just the French market which has been under siege. Do you remember I was telling you about the rumours of adding sugar to the wine in Germany? Well, I heard last night that there are prosecutions under way now.'

'So everyone's at it?'

'Not exactly. But it's quite clear that someone is capitalizing on dishonesty, someone has created a climate of doubt, a climate of distrust.'

'Didn't you say some French Minister had resigned?'

'Monsieur Figues? Yes. He went last week, on a wave of rumours that he hadn't been anxious to authorize spot checks on certain well-known wine merchants in Dijon. It wouldn't be a good scandal if at least one Cabinet Minister didn't shoot himself in the Bois de Boulogne or, at the very least, resign.' Fraser shifted position. 'But the interesting thing is that every time public interest has started to wane, something has turned up to re-kindle the imagination. You could say it was coincidence but I like to think that somewhere is the puppet-master, pulling the strings, pushing a story, kindling a rumour. It's been a story which just won't die.'

'But the wine which was switched in Bordeaux? Won't that have been tasted by someone?'

'No. The customer buys by reputation of the shipper, the vineyard, the year. If all prospective purchasers had a chance to taste the wine before buying, then there'd be none left to sell. The wine price index is already down to 109 from 162 and that's bad news for anyone who's been buying wine as an investment, bad news for companies like le Breton, with cellars full of wine.'

'Do you know, Barty, you seem to make even the most boring things sound interesting. Yes. I think I will go to the auction. I might even buy something.'

'What do you think of Henri?'

'Well, I only met him last night for the first time. It's too early to say.'

'But you do trust him, don't you?'

Emma sat up and leant forward, putting extra strain on the top part of her bikini as she did so. 'I'd never thought about it. Why do you ask?'

'No reason. Just thinking aloud. I mean, I met him under curious circumstances. I took him at face value and I've been like a limpet ever since — reliant upon him for initiatives. Maybe it's the New Orleans sun, but I was just thinking about how I could be blown off course so easily if he were feeding me wrong information.'

'You mean that Henri could be part of a cover-up, a person whose job is to keep throwing you off the scent?'

'Something like that. Just suppose the people in Burgundy had read in the papers about my involvement. They might well have done. Suppose Lucien Lubeau's mistress let slip that I'm keeping an eye on that truck in Bordeaux. So the puppet-master gets Henri Chambon to see me off.'

'But you said that he saved your life in that warehouse.'

'True!'

'Well, it's nearly time to go. You'll soon find out.'

'I thought I could trust him implicitly but, the more I think about it, the more I know that every dead end we've investigated has been one where he's reported. Every positive achievement has been one which I've suggested. That's all.' He drained the last of his champagne and stood up. 'I wonder where we'd be now if I'd never met Chambon.'

'I think you're worrying about nothing, Barty.' Unusually, her face was serious. 'You'll just have to test everything he says against your own judgment. After all, you told me that it was your idea that the fraud could be centred on California. Whatever you discover, you'll have to test against that.'

'Yes — that was my idea, or at least mine and Lucien Lubeau's. I've identified all the major California growers who are selling into Europe, who understand the French market and who are in a big enough way of business to want to cripple the French. There's just a handful of them.'

'And does Henri Chambon know all the names?'

'Yes. I've told him.'

Emma said nothing but then led the way round the pool to the awning by the lift.

Three blocks away and overlooking Jackson Square, two other men were talking. Each had a big cigar, pugnacious features and the harsh, uncompromising accents of the East Coast. At a glance, they were immediately unlikeable, but who they were and the reason for their presence could not be judged as they spoke in low tones, heads close together. In fact they were in New Orleans on orders from McMac and Great Pinewood Shores, the parent company.

'Time to go to this lousy auction,' said one.

'Sure. We gonna buy?'

'Nope. We're there to watch. Those are our orders from Atlantic City. But I sure as hell ain't sure what we're gonna see.' The elder of the two, who was aged forty, looked at his companion before continuing. 'Did I tell you our boy in New York picked up this guy Smoky Levante? He was the nigger that broad told us about.'

'That Annie Maguire woman?'

'Sure. She was the broad who hid in the cab when Zeeler was shot. She recognized Levante as the killer.'

'And Zeeler was the guy who was goin' roun' complainin' about the wine?'

'Right! She lay in the back of the cab while Levante drove her through New York.'

'What now, then?'

'By the time Rudi Ramalpo has finished with this black bastard I guess we'll know who paid him to kill off Zeeler.

And, if it's the guy I expect, then I guess we'll have orders to move in.'

'Who do they reckon it is?'

'They reckon it might be a downtown wine merchant called Joe Mocari. But there ain't no proof yet. But I guess that, after Rudi's persuasion, Levante will holler. And, if Joe Mocari's the guy who lost us these few million bucks, then I guess someone will be reading his life insurance policies pretty soon.'

Even before the last lot had been knocked down, both Fraser and Chambon had mentally eliminated most of the buyers. The hangers-on were self-evident, as were the substantial horde of journalists who, like Emma, were recording Muir Hawthorne's first auction, in the knowledge that it could be historic for all kinds of reasons. But it hadn't worked out that way at all, for the dramatic slump in European prices had not been reflected and the best wines which France could produce had all been sold, untasted, in accordance with the auctioneers' conditions, as if the word slump had never been invented.

The only lots of any interest to Fraser had been those which had arrived in the container at Savannah, ex Bordeaux, and both he and Chambon had quickly appreciated that there had been three main buyers of this wine who had been easily spotted as they bid against each other for lot after lot, pushing up prices, bringing joy to the heart of the auctioneer.

'What did you think then, Bart?' enquired Chambon as they left Canal Street behind and strolled, Emma with them, towards the river.

'I think we're down to the three people who were interested, almost obsessed, in buying the wine brought in that container. You've got their names?'

'Yes. Not without difficulty but I managed it.' They

crossed Jackson Square, thick with its usual array of artists and con-men. They climbed the steps up to the river which came into view just as the paddle-steamer *Natchez* slipped her moorings with an impressive blast of her siren. Resplendent with her red and white paintwork gleaming in the midday sun, she was in contrast to the heavy, deep, fast-flowing waters of the Mississippi. 'One bidder was an agent for a dollar millionaire from Milwaukee, the short fat guy with the bald head is a Circuit Judge from Fort Lauderdale, and the third man is called Murray Kaufmann, who comes from a Hawaiian island called Maui.'

Ever alert, Emma's head was quickly turned to face Chambon. 'A Hawaiian island, did you say?'

'Yes,' said Chambon as he selected a riverside bench, removed his formal blue tie and unbuttoned his collar.

'Barty, you told me that one of the hotel numbers you got in Sète was for a hotel in Hawaii. Coincidence?' She grinned. 'I'm not just here for my expenses, you know. Between these ears lies the greatest thing since the silicon chip.'

'Emma! You could be right.' It was Chambon who had taken up her idea. 'It fits in well with the instant pen pictures which I've built up of the three main bidders. Take the man from Milwaukee. People round the room told me that he's a well-known fanatic for French wines and was an under-bidder at Chicago when the Château Petrus reached its record level. Ever since then he's been desperate to get hold of as many first growth Bordeaux as possible. And money's no object. For the quality of the wines going under the hammer, it would have been surprising if he'd not been one of the major bidders.'

There was silence for a moment as the three of them sat appreciating the touch of breeze from the river, while the sun beat down relentlessly. Any noise around them came from the chatter of Japanese tourists and the occasional

excitable shouts of the locals as they went about their
daily routine. 'And the man from Fort Lauderdale?'
enquired Fraser.

'I don't rate him as a suspect. His name is Benjamin
Kranski. He's a Circuit Judge in Florida. For work he fills
the cells, for pleasure he fills his cellars. That's what they
say. I guess we can rule him out.'

Fraser stood, anxious to be on the move. The hot,
steamy climate seemed to play hell with his joints. 'Not
quite. I think it's dangerous to eliminate anyone.' Even as
he was speaking, he was thinking once again of his
conversation with Emma, yet hating himself for doing so,
for Chambon seemed trustworthy but he must never allow
his judgment to be blinkered or conditioned solely by the
Frenchman. He must stand apart, test everything against
his own view and make up his own mind. 'What about the
third man. The one from Hawaii?'

'His name is Murray Kaufmann. No one seemed to
know much about him. Give me half an hour and a few
phone calls and I'll have him taped.'

'Make it an hour,' said Fraser. 'I'd like to take a shower,
shake off the heat of the morning and then meet you for
lunch. Shall we say two-thirty in the Court of the Two
Sisters? I'm feeling really pooped with all this heat.'

'Me too,' said Emma, looking as cool as a primrose in
mountain dew in her lemon trouser suit. Hand in hand,
Fraser and Emma set off for their hotel, leaving Chambon
to use his contacts to find out a little more of the life-style
of Murray Kaufmann.

It was nearly an hour and a half later when they returned
to the cool leafy shade of the Court of the Two Sisters.
Fraser's much-needed shower had turned into an erotic
experience as Emma had joined him and had insisted on
hiding the soap in the most unlikely places, until his
interest had been irretrievably aroused. 'Henri can wait,'

had been Emma's final exhortation as she had led him
back to the bedroom.

'You're late,' chided the Frenchman, as he rose to greet
them. 'I'm on to my third drink already. Shall we go
straight in?' He was not to be denied and the three of
them went straight through to the courtyard, where most
of the diners were approaching the end of their meal.
They sat down close to the fountain and Chambon was
quick to get to the point.

'Whilst you two have been . . . cooling off, I've got a
few facts sorted out about our friend Murray Kaufmann.
He's an acknowledged expert, a Wine Master, a former
chief enologist who worked on a vineyard in the Napa
Valley. He was a graduate of the University of California
but went into retirement last year on Maui. He's never
been known to buy wine at auction before, but if he were
to challenge the authenticity of a wine, then no question
he's got the ear of the world straight away.'

'So someone, as yet unknown, arranged for him to buy
the wine and then criticize it . . .' Fraser left the thought
in the air.

'Exactly. If an amateur was unimpressed with a bottle
of 1961 claret then . . . so what? But if Murray Kaufmann
breaks into print that a bottle of 1961 Château Lafite is
nothing of the kind, then the ultimate wine investment is
lost and gone for ever. It'll end up cheaper than Coke and
he can get back-up for his views from anywhere. He's a
pretty neat choice.'

'So what now?' enquired Emma.

'We find out just what makes Murray Kaufmann tick,
with whom he deals, to whom he talks, because whoever it
is will be the puppet-master.' Again it was Chambon who
was doing the positive thinking, Fraser who was latching
on, yet the logic of the agent's approach seemed
impeccable. He felt guilty that he'd even harboured
doubts as he and Chambon raised their glasses of red wine

to each other, in acknowledgement of what they'd achieved. Emma, for her part, was happily pouring champagne from the bucket which stood beside her.

'By the way,' she said, 'my Editor will be pleased. I saw the Earl of Trasker at the auction. And the blonde he was with was certainly not his wife. That titbit alone will get my expenses paid by the paper.'

'Or five pounds from the Editor of *Private Eye!*' laughed Fraser. He was about to continue in the same bantering tone when Chambon motioned him to be silent, his smile wolfish, his cheeks tight, eyes narrow under the thin eyebrows.

'I have a little confession to make to you both.' Confident that he'd attracted their interest, Chambon continued. 'I can tell you why you can rule out that fourth man, the one from Houston who was doing some bidding but always ended up the under-bidder. You see, I planted him.'

'You did?' Fraser's face showed incredulity.

'*Mais oui!* Besides wanting to frame whoever's behind all this, my instructions were to ensure that prices were high, so I'd arranged for eight people to be in the hall, all bidding up the prices, creating the impression that confidence had returned to the French wine market. But it hasn't. If you think about it, the traditional big buyers were slow to come forward and rapidly withdrew as prices started to soar. An illusion of strength in the market was created which was never there.'

'You're a crafty old bugger,' said Fraser.

'I'll drink to that. Isn't that what you say in England?'

# NEW YORK

With Emma close beside him, Bart Fraser was settling down to an evening of jazz, among the spartan surroundings of Preservation Hall in New Orleans. Lunch, in the sophistication of the Court of the Two Sisters, had been long and leisurely and had left them replete for the evening.

Pete Dixon's Spaghetti House in New York, where Joe Mocari was spending his evening sitting alone, was in stark contrast. Despite his substantial income and the expectation of huge fortunes to come, Mocari still remained faithful to Pete. He had been dining there for so long that he hadn't noticed where the emulsion was peeling back from the walls with the damp, had failed to notice that the once-white walls were now yellowed and stained by years of nicotine. Mocari noticed only the generous helpings, the warmth of the atmosphere and a lifelong friendship with the owner.

In front of him, on the formica table, was his usual glass of water, cup of coffee and a mountain of spaghetti and meatballs, his favourite meal. But his thoughts were elsewhere as he ate and then mechanically wiped up the last dregs of greasy meat from the greyish-white of the plate. Already he was looking forward to his cigarette, debating whether to visit his favourite whorehouse in Lafayette Street or take in a movie, a dilemma improved because there was no need to make a choice. He could do both. In any order he chose.

The small steamy room was quiet, for he was eating later than most of the patrons. It was Pete Dixon's night off and there was no one to talk to, so he stared, gazing at the print of Lake Como. He'd never been there, come to that, didn't know where it was. And no more did Pete Dixon neither.

Unaware that Smoky had been identified by Annie Maguire, been found by Rudi Ramalpo, and had saved his own life by naming Mocari, the diner pushed back his chair, paid his bill and left.

'Tell Pete I'll be in tomorrow night.'

Outside, in the darkened street, the air was warm. Mocari slipped off his jacket and draped it over his right shoulder and started to walk in the direction of Lafayette Street, knowing that subconsciously his decision had already been taken. He hoped that Rosie would be free. She seemed to have that way of bringing him on real good, of making him feel wanted, never giving him any hint of the others who had paid their fifty bucks for their thirty minutes in the saddle.

The streets were busy, full of people, shopping for pastrami, salami or pizzas. From all around came the sound of music filling the air with lilting Italian melodies. Yes! Life was good and to be enjoyed. And Rosie was only two blocks away now. He looked to his left to cross the road and was immediately aware of a dark green Mustang, somewhat battered, which accelerated from about twenty yards behind him. It drew level and pulled up. One glance through the windows was enough for him to read his epitaph written on the faces within.

The back door of the car opened and instantly he was bundled inside, where he sat, a fifteen stoner on one side of him and a larger man on the other, a gun pressed into his ribs. In a few moments the vehicle was speeding across Brooklyn Bridge, leaving behind the towering lights of the Manhattan skyscrapers. The car stopped in a side street full of red brick tenements, their façades spoiled by the repeated zig-zags of fire escapes. Into one building Mocari was hustled and, within moments, stripped even of his red and white boxer trunks, and then bound, naked, to what appeared to be an operating table. Above him a spotlight shone in his face, blurring his awareness of the surroundings or of the faces which were watching him. All he knew was that there were three men there, two of whom had bound him with leather thongs by ankles and wrists. It was the third man who spoke.

'Thought you'd have known better, Joe.' The voice was nasal and sneering and the use of the Christian name did not mean that Mocari knew the identity of the speaker. 'You've been costin' us a few million bucks. Been out to break us. Three million bottles in McMac. Ripped the guts out of our vineyard in France. Nearly ruined us. But you should have known better than that, Joe. We don't break. It's you that breaks.'

'I dunno what you're on about.' Mocari was surprised at how defiant he sounded.

'Don't give us that crap! We know you hired Smoky Levante to get rid of your front man Hubert Zeeler. And he did. But he didn't know that Zeeler's girl-friend was there and saw him. And she identified him, 'cos she didn't like her guy being murdered by the shits he'd been working for. Even more, when he wasn't paid for it. Like, you were so greedy that you had him shot before he was paid. Now that wasn't nice, was it, Joe? And when we spoke to Smoky, he didn't think it was that nice neither, 'specially after we spoke to him . . . in this very room.' The speaker walked round Mocari's prostrate body. 'And so Smoky told us who hired him and we had a chat. He was really rather sensible. Told us everything he knew, including all about the man who hired him. And that's where you come in.'

'You've got it all wrong. I don't know any Smoky. Say, who the hell is he?'

They ignored him. 'Who's your partner? I'm counting to ten. Then the pain starts.' Mocari thought quickly, thought of Coburn's determination to go ahead with

McMac's, despite the obvious risk to his New York partner. Had Coburn ensured that McMac's hoods would catch him, eliminate him? Maybe. It wasn't easy to be certain with a spotlight dazzling one's vision, with three men hovering close at hand. Sweat cascaded from his fat, hairy and undesirable body, dripped between his buttocks, oozed from his armpits, saturated his chest. One thing was certain: there was no fun in being a dead hero, not least for Nat Coburn, not for Coburn who had gone ahead, not caring about the risks or the consequences to his erstwhile friend, Joseph H. Mocari.

Mocari flinched as he sensed his captors closing around him. Something *very* painful was seconds away. 'You want to say something, Joe?'

'Coburn. Nat Coburn.' As he spat out the name Mocari felt a surge of relief. Time to look after himself. 'Minstrel Creek Winery. Monterey.'

'We kinda thought it might be him.'

'Can I go now?'

'Sure,' said Ramalpo. 'You can go to hell.' The .32 bullet was fired in contact with the centre of Mocari's forehead and the force of discharge on to the scalp split the entry wound. Death was instantaneous and had come exactly as Mocari had predicted.

'Get rid of him, Lex. Make sure he's never discovered.'


MAUI, HAWAII


The Cessna dipped its port wing and circled over the intense blue of the Pacific. Looking out of the window, Fraser searched for the airstrip of the tiny blob of island, the jewel of the Hawaiian cluster. Then he saw it—and strip it was, a thin line, just wide enough for light aircraft, hewn from the lines of the Ka'anapali sugar plantations.

Along the shore were the first signs that progress and commercialism were only as far away as the nearest entrepreneur but, inland, the verdant depths of the island looked unspoiled, ready to elevate the spirits of the long-distance traveller.

'Not quite Heathrow.' Fraser grinned at Emma, as the pilot, with laconic experience of countless troublefree trips, swooped down and parked beside the delightfully small terminal building. 'Heathrow,' repeated Fraser. 'Remember? Where you ought to be right now.'

'The hours I put in, the Editor owes me a few days off. Besides—I'm on the verge of a scoop.'

'Maybe.' Fraser was thoughtful, uncertain as to how to respond.

Emma jumped out and stood for a moment, savouring the luxurious fragrance of the warm air. 'These small planes,' she enthused. 'That was just great! Really brought out the Amy Johnson in me. Oh look! There's a bar in the terminal. Let's have a drink.'

'I thought it was me who had the drink problem.' Though he could joke about it, his longing for alcohol was still too strong. He knew that.

'I just fancy some champagne. Lots of it and then lots of romping at the hotel.'

'We're here to work.' The reprimand was meant to be ignored, as he knew it would be.

'We'll drink to the health of my Editor.'

'Not exactly happy with your report of the auction, was he? All that stuff about the bidders being bow-tied, beau-jollied poofters. Not exactly why he sent you four thousand miles from London, was it?'

'But he's *using* the piece. It just needed a little bit of editing.' She flicked her hair dismissively, tossing aside any shred of care for what the Editor thought anyway. 'I think he was quite pleased, really.' She pulled Fraser by the hand. 'Come on. It's called Harry's Windsock Bar. It's up these stairs.' Nimbly she climbed the tightly spiralled staircase which led from the ground floor to the only upper room of the terminal.

'How you doing, sir!' The genuine pleasure oozed from the barman's friendly greeting as Fraser reached the top. 'Isn't it just a great day for doing sweet FA. That'll be two Bloody Marys.'

'Champagne.' Emma's reaction was predictable.

'Suit yourself, only everyone here drinks Bloody Marys. It's the house speciality.' A glance round the tiny room revealed that the only two other customers were drinking the speciality and were nodding approval. Fraser doubted their judgment as the colour of their eyes and complexion was more than a match for the mixture in front of them.

'OK. We give in.'

'You won't regret it. First visit to Maui, is it?'

'Yes. We've just flown from New Orleans via L.A.' Fraser was looking round the walls, thick with visiting cards, photographs, treasury notes from every nation, faded and curled by the passage of time on an island which had seemed timeless. 'Drink and enjoy,' commanded the barman.

'We sure will,' Emma responded, slipping into the American style as readily as a chameleon. They chatted inconsequentially as their glasses rapidly emptied and Fraser watched the gentle roll of the Pacific on the hot sand, his mind on the hold which Emma now had on him. Yet his instinct was to shy away, for she was everything which he was not.

'Daydreaming again?' He was stirred from his thoughts as she pinched his arm. 'Mr Windsock here was enquiring whether you wanted another drink.'

'Sorry. Yes, I'll have another. But it'll be the last. We've got to get on.'

The barman reached again for the vodka but continued talking while he was working. 'Did you know that Maui has been described as Paradise? Someone described it as the '*Last place on Earth*'. Well, I don't know about that but I sure hope it's the last place which most folk find. We don't want to see no more change. There's enough right now. You been to Waikiki?'

'No. We changed planes at Honolulu but didn't stop there at all.'

'Right. Don't bother, folks. Like, it's a real turn-off. Round Waikiki Beach the murder rate's doubled in ten years. The whole place is cheap, tacky, full of hookers, junkies and muggers. Did they teach you at school that there are more hotel rooms in Waikiki than in New York City? No—I bet they didn't.' He produced the drinks. 'Honolulu's full of people and canned pineapple. Keep the pineapple—can the people, that's my slogan.'

'I don't think we'll bother to go there, shall we?' Emma loved Fraser's understatement, so alien to her own exuberance.

'There's been some development here,' continued the barman. 'But it's mainly for the fat cats. You'll see. Where are you staying? The Hyatt?'

'No. Up at Wailea.'

The barman nodded. 'Sure. Good choice. Can't go wrong. Just a pity it's the wrong time of year. You've missed the whales.'

'Whales? You have whales here?'

'Between December and May every year. We get maybe five hundred humpbacks cavorting.'

'Why do they come here?'

'To make love, to roll about, to enjoy themselves.'

'Sounds like us,' said Emma as she leant across to slip her hand inside Fraser's beach shirt. A month ago he'd have been embarrassed, uneasy, concerned about the reaction of others. Now he knew better, able to enjoy the fun of the moment as the room filled with laughter.

'Say, did you ever hear of Murray Kaufmann?' asked Fraser.

'Murray Kaufmann? Sure, I've heard. Lives at Wailea. Not far from your hotel. You got a car booked?'

'Yes. We'll have to be going.'

As they went to descend the staircase, which seemed to spiral even tighter than ever now, the barman continued his tirade against Waikiki to the remaining customers. 'Over at Waikiki Beach everything's canned: the music, the food, the pineapple. Come to think of it, even the people are canned. One day, when I'm Emperor of *all* the Islands, then I'll give them a can. It'll be the most goddamned big trash can you ever did see in your doggoned life.'

Murray Kaufmann's villa was hard by the hotel. Had it been on the most exclusive estate, then access would have been impossible, for that particular development was guarded by sentries, day and night, like Aldershot barracks. In contrast, Kaufmann's property stood expensively alone on rising ground, looking out across a thin, sandy strip to thousands of miles of empty ocean. It was the home of a connoisseur, selected, just like his wines, with enormous attention to detail.

'Our friend Mr Kaufmann's done well,' commented Emma.

'As long as his liver lasts he can enjoy quite a view, but educated palates and an early slab in the morgue are irresistibly linked.'

'You should know.'

'No way. There's no way I'm going back to that. In fact, what I'm going to do is work so hard that I can fill a piggy-bank and buy a house like this. It's quite something.'

'Gold-plated taps, I'd guess. The only question is, how Kaufmann got the money.'

'Is he a pawn or has he been used?'

'Henri should know. We've got to trust him,' said Fraser, shaking a tree in the fruitless hope of releasing a coconut. 'To tell the truth, I'm regretting my doubts.'

'But he's got a different viewpoint.'

'Yes.' Fraser spoke slowly, as he thought about the observation. 'His goals and ours aren't necessarily at the same end but that isn't to say that he'd score an own goal.'

'But from whom does he get instructions?'

'Somebody pretty desperate. He won't say precisely. He's being paid to get results and without publicity. *We're* looking for justice, or even vengeance: anything to restore the reputation of Giles le Breton. Yes.' He tugged his ear. 'We need Henri because of his connections. We've got no choice.'

'Sounds a bit heavy to me. Let's go have a drink,' Emma replied. 'Say! I'm talking American again. Get that! Now ain't that just cute.'

In their hotel, fearfully potent Mai-tais in front of them, they waited and waited still longer for Henri Chambon. He'd arrived on the island two days earlier. When he joined them, his face was smiling, his small body lost inside a multi-coloured shirt and purple trousers. Nevertheless, as he was no more badly dressed than anyone else in Hawaii, he was certainly not conspicuous. Having kissed them lavishly, with much smacking of lips, he took a seat on the verandah and ordered a Scotch.

'Anything to tell me?' he asked, without any pretence of interest in small talk.

'We've done rather well,' said Fraser. 'We've found Murray Kaufmann's villa. Cased it, I think is the jargon.' Emma nodded her head in agreement.

'You've done well,' enthused the Frenchman. 'You've really cased it? You know where to get in, where the burglar alarm is, where the cellars can be found? Is that right?'

'It's impregnable. Like Fort Knox.'

'You think so?'

'Yes. You'll never get into there.'

'Quite right.' Chambon's face was a mask.

'How have you been getting on?' enquired Fraser.

'Fairly well, I think. As you know, I went to Savannah and a question or two in the right places confirmed the flights taking the wine to the buyers. Monsieur Kaufmann's wine was due for delivery yesterday.'

'And did it arrive?'

'Yes.'

'And?' Fraser was sure that there was more to come.

'Not a lot. Nothing really, except that the previous day his phone was neatly bugged.'

'Bugged!' Emma almost shouted the word in surprise.

Chambon grinned, at the same time suggesting that she should keep her voice down. 'But yes. It was easy really. A contact of mine in Honolulu got in and bugged the phone.'

'You mean he . . . broke in?'

'Oh no. As you said, the place is impregnable. There's no way he could break in.'

'So what did he do?'

'Waited till Mr Kaufmann was out and then walked through the front door. And it's simple. All you need is an Autopik.'

'An Autopik!' squealed Emma. 'What's that?'

'Just about the simplest gadget for undoing locks. There are two types and Kaufmann's house was fitted with a rather rare type of cylinder lock which made it necessary to use a rake gun, rather than the pik gun which handles the more simple locks. Not a burglar alarm went off. He simply walked in, went straight to the phones and fitted some bugs.'

In her job, Emma was used to hanging around outside third-floor bedrooms in Chelsea in the hope of catching a tête-à-tête between a Lord or a Lady, but the actual use of illicit surveillance material was another world.

'You look shocked! You shouldn't be. The people I represent are fighting a war, a fight for survival. Illegal wire-tapping is pretty widespread.' Chambon smiled. 'In fact, I should check your own phone when you get back. Journalists' phones are always being tapped.' Chambon was pleased when he saw the surprised look intensify, so he continued: 'It's the work of only a few moments to fit a "drop-in" device. It's just a tiny microphone/radio-transmitter. This particular one was broadcasting on ninety-four megacycles, on what you know as the VHF band. One mile away, in his van, my contact was able to listen to every call made or received from that moment onwards.'

'And was it interesting?' In the heat of the chase, Fraser's duties as a solicitor had long been forgotten. Somehow it didn't seem so bad to break the law in another country.

'We know there's a crisis meeting tonight down at Murray Kaufmann's house. He spoke to someone. Said there was a problem.'

'Who's the man?'

'We should find out in two hours' time. My colleague will take photographs when the gentleman arrives and we'll be at the Hyatt, making use of our other little toy.' Knowing that he had their attention, he paused to sip his drink.

'Get on with it, Henri. Explain yourself,' said Emma.

'Kaufmann has two phones. In each there's a combined telephone tap and room bugging device. All I have to do is to dial Kaufmann's number from my hotel room. His telephone doesn't ring. Instead, the rooms in which there is a phone become live and any conversation in that room, or on that telephone, can be heard.'

'My God! I didn't think it was possible.' Fraser shook his head in disbelief.

'It's not only possible — it's commonplace. So, before tonight's out, we're going to be considerably wiser.'

'But we can't use that evidence — not if it's illegal,' retorted Fraser.

'No. But there's no doubt we can use it to our advantage. Must be able to. Anyway, I'm not necessarily going to the police.'

Seemingly nonchalant, Nat Coburn strolled out of the Hyatt Hotel. His hire-car which had been valet parked was pleasantly cool. He wasn't due at Murray Kaufmann's for another hour, but inside he was boiling, his nerves on edge, his mind anguished in frustration. What *was* going on? As he joined the highway, a small, red saloon, with two men and a pretty blonde passed him but the occupants of neither car took any notice of the other although, had they but known, an opportunity for some mutual explanations would have been possible. As it was, Chambon led the others to his room, where they sat on the balcony, gazing down at the spectacular garden full of exotic birds and mysterious paths eight floors below.

Within minutes of starting his journey darkness descended on Maui, and where moments before there had been the warm evening glow from the sunset, now Coburn's route was lit only by the headlamps. Not that he'd appreciated the fiery redness of the sky as the sun had dropped rapidly into the Pacific; not that Coburn had noticed that every branch of every tree, of every wave on every beach had been delicately tinted by the intensity of the sunset. As he drove, his eyes were restless, his normally calm face puckered and his teeth chewing at his lower lip.

After his arrival on the Royal Hawaiian Air Service

flight, he'd even ignored the array of sunburnt beauties sprawled around the tumbling waters of the swimming pools. Something was on his mind — something even more important to him than the caress of a breast. It was money, the need for it, the drive for it, the lust for it, and the concern that something, something intangible and not readily explained, was sniping at the plans which had gone so well.

The road was narrow, predominantly straight and flat, as it ran round the edge of the shore, occasionally giving glimpses of peaceful bays. But he didn't see them. Kaufmann had certainly sounded alarmed and confused when he had phoned. Urgent, he had said; you must get here, he had said. And yet why? Surely nothing could have gone wrong? The reports from France had been positive. The switch had taken place. The wine had been shipped and Kaufmann had purchased classic wines at classic prices. The scene had been set for Kaufmann's expert attack; an attack which would be the final broadside in the campaign to destroy the reputation of the European wine market.

It had all gone so well. Every magazine, both in Europe and America, to say nothing of all the major newspapers, had continued to up-date story after story, upgrading rumours into facts, and facts into pernicious legend. Only the high prices achieved at the New Orleans auction had been a puzzlement. But the higher the prices, the greater the outrage when exposure arrived and anyway there was no accounting for speculators and wine buffs.

The disappearance of Joe Mocari had not been unexpected. The New York wine dealer had been well paid for his assistance and his absence was a matter of little moment. Perhaps he was now in hiding.

Neither had there been any feedback from Europe on the deaths of the van drivers. Nowhere had it been suggested that the deaths were anything other than they had appeared. No one had suggested that the attacks on the French wine industry had been orchestrated, and all the while the sales of French wine had been falling, leaving the conventional trade overladen with wine which was difficult to value and even more difficult to sell.

Of course the Californian wine market had not been the only one to benefit. The Australians, with their wines from the Hunter Valley, had been quick to see the opportunity and so had the occasional exporter from Chile, but nowhere had been better placed and better financed to capitalize on the European discomfort than the richly endowed vineyards of California. Innocent and entirely unaware of what Coburn was doing, the great names of California like Mondavi, Christian Brothers and Masson, had been able to use their experience and expertise to push for that bigger share of the European market.

There'd been intruders at the warehouse in Sète, but that had been weeks ago, and whoever it had been had stolen nothing, had caused no trouble. Yet it was a puzzlement, a niggle he could do without.

But now this? What was Kaufmann on about? He'd expected the expert's complaint to be news by the following day, to be the talk of every grower, of every merchant, of every Minister in every Department in France. There would be calls for Public Inquiries, takeover bids, and heads would surely roll.

He opened the window and threw out a stub end of cigar, as the lights of Wailea appeared and he quickly found the archway, leading into Kaufmann's ranch-style property. The short drive was stony and bounded on each side by luxuriant bushes and shrubs. By the front door was Kaufmann's Cadillac, bathed in the floodlights which lit the entire property as a safeguard against felons.

As he got out of the car, the last thing on Coburn's mind was the possibility that he was being watched, was being photographed with a rapid-fire series of clicks by an observer hidden in the shadows near the arch.

Even before he had knocked at the door, it was opened by Kaufmann, his plump face and balding head pinkened by the Hawaiian sun. His rimless glasses sat on the end of a strawberry nose which, however extraordinary in appearance, could nevertheless identify a wine to its country, its region, and frequently its very vineyard and year. He had the face, the air, of a man who had spent a life of relative relaxation. There was not a line on it despite his fifty-five years, but tonight, though he wore the most casual clothes, his greeting, though friendly, was restrained.

The door closed behind the two men and the photographer slipped away, his task concluded. Mug shots of them both? He had plenty.

A few moments earlier Chambon had direct dialled Murray Kaufmann's number, but in place of the strident ring in the Wailea villa, the electronic tone oscillator prevented the slightest sound. Instead, the microphones in Kaufmann's leather-chaired study were all ears. The telephone, standing on his desk, quiet and innocent, was now hearing and transmitting every noise from the comfortable opulence of the room to the listener twenty-five miles away.

'We've got him.' Chambon nodded his head as the tape-recorder by his feet started to operate.

'I can't hear anything,' said Fraser, craning forward.

'No. Not yet. But I can tell that the room's live. The meeting's not due to start for another five minutes. There are only two telephones. One in the study and one in a bedroom.'

The remains of giant open roast beef sandwiches lay in front of them, together with a nearly empty bottle of Diamond Creek wine. Emma's face was alert and shining, her hands trembling slightly at the adventure of it all. In contrast, Bart Fraser looked calm, the only sign of nervousness being an excess of swallowing and a repeated, absent-minded scratching of his left elbow.

Suddenly there were voices coming through their receiver and into the tape-recorder, just as if the speakers were talking to them personally. Chambon raised a finger.

'You want a drink, Nat?'

'Fix me a Manhattan, would you. On the Rocks.'

From somewhere came the sound of movement and what might have been the tinkling of ice cubes into a glass. Chambon looked up. 'Nat — is it? Won't be too hard to check that name out.'

'Well, it sure is a nice place you've got here, Murray, but I guess you didn't ask me to leave my vineyard and come two thousand miles just for the view.'

'I guess not. We've got a problem.'

'Like what?'

'Like there ain't nothing wrong with this wine.' There was a clinking of bottles. 'As you can see, I've opened several. Now I needn't tell you, Nat, that wines suffer from jet-lag just as much as you and me. But hell, Nat, these wines are as near perfect as any wine I've tasted.'

'Shit! But that's impossible. It's goddamned impossible, Murray.' There was a long silence. 'Are you sure?'

'Yeah. Sure I'm sure. Here — you taste it.' There was a sound of movement and then silence.

'See what you mean. Now, this is the Château Cheval Blanc 1961. Hell, Murray, I've got to agree with you. No one ain't gonna believe you if you say there's anything wrong with that. That wine is as beautiful as I've ever tasted. The colour, the bouquet, the legs round the glass. All perfect.'

'That's why I asked you over here, Nat. You told me the wine would be trash, that anyone would believe me.'

'That's what I thought.'

'So what's your game, Nat?' Again there was a silence but the same voice continued after a pause. 'I've been thinking, Nat, were you trying to discredit me? Trying to make me a fool, saying this French wine was no good, when you knew it was?'

'Come off it, Murray. Would I do that?'

'I don't know. I wouldn't have thought so but that's what I've been thinking today.'

'Jesus Leroy Christ! Quit it, Murray! You know that ain't my game. Can't you find any fault? Not in any of them, for Chrissake! I mean, we're all geared up to give a press statement. It's the final round — discrediting the auction. This game ain't been for peanuts, you know that. There's two hundred and fifty new acres of vines back in Monterey and I've borrowed every cent to pay for them. If I don't get no big return this year, then . . .' The voice was cut off by the listener.

'I know, Nat, but this balls-up ain't my fault. I agreed to help. You made it worth my while. So I buy some wine at auction. You tell me it's going to be crap. You want me to say so, tell the Press and back it up. Everyone will believe me and other experts who taste it are bound to agree. And now this. Just about the most beautiful selection of cases of wine I've ever bought. That Château Palmer 1975. You could drink that in fifteen years' time and it'll still be great. And the Chambertin, it's perfection. Don't ask me to explain, Nat, but I guess you've been screwed.'

'You some kind of genius, Murray? So, just cut out the crap. You was some kind of Professor. It's about time you started thinking like one. Bounce a few ideas off the wall. And no more crap, eh Murray?'

The listeners heard nothing for a few seconds. 'I think it's time for you to go, Nat. I agreed to help. I didn't agree to be insulted. Nobody, including you, is going to make an asshole out of me.' Kaufmann's voice was shouting now. 'You finish that drink. You just get out. I can live without creeps like you.'

'If you say so, Murray. But don't forget that little incident at the so-called blind tasting in San Francisco. One word from you, Murray, and your name will be in every gossip column. Sure, and the State police will be paying you a little visit.' Coburn let the threat hang and mature for a moment. 'I suggest you just sit here the rest of your days and drink yourself to death.' The listeners heard the voice fade away. 'I'll see myself out.'

In Chambon's room at the Hyatt, the three of them looked at each other as Chambon replaced the receiver. 'So! Nat, whoever he is, owns a vineyard in California. Might be Nat Coburn. He was on the list. We'll wait for the photographs. After that, it'll be easy.'

Emma looked puzzled. 'I don't understand.'

Fraser looked across at Chambon for confirmation before speaking. Gently he leant forward so that he could see the fine downy hair on her pale pink cheeks. 'Just could be,' he said, 'that someone switched back the containers in the yard at Bordeaux.'

Emma's eyes widened in amazement. 'You?'

Fraser's grin was from ear to ear. 'Not just me, of course. And it was Henri's idea. He managed to get some keys to the trucks. Then we climbed into the yard through the window.'

'And of course we changed the number plates,' added Chambon, making the word 'changed' sound very splashy in his otherwise perfect English. 'In the morning there was no way that the drivers could know what had happened. I rather thought that it might cause some confusion, and listening to Coburn fall out with his pal rather proves my point. What's more, we've safeguarded the reputation of the French wine growers into the bargain.'

'You might have told me.' Emma looked hurt for a moment. Then she raised her glass. 'I'm going to drink to two of the most devious people I've ever met. But what now?'

'When we've identified Nat?' Chambon thought for a moment. 'We'll visit him. I think we can sort this one out.'

'But what about the cops?'

'Not yet. Wait till we've seen this guy Nat. I want to get him to come clean — in public. Force him to put his publicity machine into reverse again.'

## CALIFORNIA

Unnoticed in the usual throng of traffic, six trucks headed south from San Francisco on Freeway 101 towards Monterey County, a hundred miles away. Just behind was a dark green le Baron saloon, the convoy arranged by Rudi Ramalpo, on instructions from Louis Spiggola of Great Pinewood Shores, Inc.

In the hypnotic glare of oncoming lights, Ramalpo's thoughts were not just of his instructions but also of the audacity of Coburn for spraying shit at a company with a Wall Street quotation. But if it went well, Ramalpo knew he'd be OK; all right for the rest of his days. The rest of his days? A smirk crossed his face. At thirty-two, an actuary would give him pretty good odds for a long life until he knew his occupation, for death in bed was a luxury which he'd never contemplated, aware that his end could be just as violent, just as unpleasant as Joe Mocari's.

He turned on the radio. Count Basie. Yes. That would do. He turned down the air-conditioning. The car felt chilly as the last of the daylight disappeared.

*

As Ramalpo's convoy headed south, the Chevette driven by Bart Fraser was approaching Nat Coburn's winery from Los Angeles. Beside him was Emma and in the back was Henri Chambon, snoozing quietly despite what lay ahead.

After an early start they'd spent the evening at Santa Barbara, not saying much, each over-aware of the confrontation with Coburn, fixed for 6.30 a.m.

On the pretext that she and Fraser were writing an article on Californian wine, Emma had telephoned Coburn for an appointment, explaining that she was an expert on profiles and Fraser the expert on wine. They would be accompanied by their photographer, a Monsieur Chambon, and their aim was to do a splash on Coburn's vineyard, with a profile on the man himself.

'I wish you'd told him we wanted to do half a day in his life,' muttered Fraser as Chambon started to snore gently. 'Then we could have had a decent sleep instead of this long flog through the night.'

'A half day in the life?' Emma laughed. 'Doesn't have the same ring about it. Nat Coburn's day starts early. I wasn't to know that.'

'Early! Is that what you call it. I seem to spend all my time either sitting in cars or contorted in jumbo seats, trying to get comfortable. I wouldn't mind getting my leg up.'

'Talk about leg-over and I might be interested.' She leant across and gave him a patronizing tap on the head. 'You're so old, you're falling apart. Dry rot in your wooden leg. Any more complaints and you'll have me crying as I spend your pension money.'

'I'll ignore that.' His voice changed. 'Being serious, you realize this could be rough? Coburn's out to sink the entire French wine trade and it's just the three of us standing in the way. He's not going to like it.'

She nodded. 'Don't let's think about it. Change the subject. But is it really necessary, checking the vines at six-thirty every morning?'

'Yes. There'll be all sorts of decisions to be taken. Is it too hot, too cold, too wet or too dry? Do the vines need some fertilizer, some chemical spray against fungus or disease. And so it goes on.'

'And he knows his job?'

'Apparently. The vineyard's expanded quite a bit, producing fairly passable wines which he's been exporting to Europe. He has to decide when the grape harvest will start.'

'Is timing that critical?' Emma was interested.

'Only to the nearest minute.' Fraser grinned from his sun-bronzed face. 'The Californians have got wine-making down to a scientific art. Mainly the soil here was right, but the climate was less than perfect. So what have they done? Only taken steps to control the weather! If it's too hot, they blow cool air across the valleys, perhaps using fans blowing over huge lumps of ice. If it's too cold, then they spray the grapes with water, which freezes, providing an overcoat for the grape itself.' Fraser nodded his head with some reverence. 'With that kind of determination, these Californians deserve their success.'

'But determination's not been enough for Coburn.' They fell silent until Emma brightened. 'But we've out-smarted him twice—once with the re-switching and once at the auction with the planted bidders.'

'Thanks to Henri—and not to me.'

'Don't you believe it, Barty.' Emma's voice was deliberate and reassuring.

'I hope you're right. But without Henri, the growers of France would have been nailed to the floor by now. Worse than that, they'd have been six feet under. Finished. Stone Dead.'

'But what I don't understand is why people would

believe that famous French vineyards would trot out
rubbish bottles for a prestige auction.'

'*I* understand. Not because it makes sense but because,
in the absence of any better explanation, and with the air
of crisis and uncertainty, the whole French wine trade is
tottering. What you need is public confidence, a belief in
the integrity of your label, especially when you're paying
sixty quid a bottle. Coburn understood this and turned it
to his advantage.'

'Sixty quid a bottle! Remind me not to spill any. It
makes my champagne sound cheap.'

Fraser twisted in his seat. 'Nothing about you is cheap.
Never will be.' They fell silent as the car cruised at a
steady 55 m.p.h. through the darkness. Emma had
nodded off.

'Mr Coburn?' Fraser stretched out a hand as the man
nodded. 'My name's Alan Dixon. And this is Emma Fry-
Cripps, from London's *Daily Topic*.' Fraser turned again.
'And this is our photographer, Monsieur Chambon. It's
kind of you to see us.'

'Good to meet you and I guess you'd like a coffee, but
you're going to be out of luck. I want to get to the vines
straight away. We'll have coffee when we get back.' He
led them towards a bright red Range-Rover. 'You want to
see a day in my life, so this is where it starts.' He pointed
out his long, low, adobe-style home, pure white with
delicate archways and intricate wrought-ironwork. The
south-facing wall was heavy with flowers of all colours. To
its side was a swimming pool, with patio and fountain.
'I'm home most of the time and, when I am, my day starts
now. Six-thirty.'

As he was talking, Emma was jotting down a pen
picture. Early thirties, well-built and without an ounce of
fat. A six-footer, good-looking, with something spine-
chilling in the features, in the blend of narrowing eyes

and sucked-in cheeks. And, just as she had been looking at him, she'd noticed him eyeing her up and down, mentally reducing her to nakedness, a rating of ten and fit for a nooner. Falling for him wouldn't be difficult, she decided.

'I guess I'm kinda rusty at these conducted tours. We get visitors most every day. One of the guys shows them round. So you'd better excuse me if I don't have the patter.' The listeners knew only too well that Nat Coburn had all the patter, despite his protestations. He swung the car on to the tarmac road. 'To our right, you can see the winery itself. Not everyone has one. Not everyone has one this big.' As they looked, they saw a series of giant stainless steel vats, each standing all of fifty feet high, lined up like soldiers in a row. 'Everything's there, crushing, fermenting, storing and bottling. It's quite something, isn't it? And we've room to expand.'

Chambon took a photograph through the open window. 'Most impressive,' said Fraser, choosing to emphasize his Queen's English. 'How many acres do you have? I haven't seen a single vine yet.'

'Well, I guess we have more than a thousand acres now. Started with three hundred but we just keep on growing. Things were pretty difficult back in 1974. You may remember there was a slump. Well, our borrowing had been geared to the prices of the early 1970's but the 1974 drop knocked most everyone sideways. But we rode it — got ourselves re-financed with big money and then kept on expanding.'

'Monterey certainly is a beautiful county. The rolling hills, these valleys . . .'

'Emma, you're right.' Coburn's familiarity came easily. 'Some vineyards owned by the majors are pretty much on the flat but it sure is something else up here.'

'Is a thousand acres big?' enquired Emma.

'Nope. It's a fair size but there's plenty controlling ten

thousand acres and more.' By now the Range-Rover had left the buildings behind and was winding along a tarmac estate road, through attractively undeveloped fields. 'I guess there'll be vines here by 1985. Now this road we're on is the main feeder to the network of our vines. Made it ourselves. Like all these roads.' As he was talking they crested a lush hilltop and, ahead of them, the landscape changed and the view was of endless vines, line upon line, regimented with almost military precision, dipping down the lengthening slope of the valley.

'Is that water over there?' enquired Fraser.

'You're right, boy. Now that water is our own reservoir which we built ourselves. Let's stop while I tell you about it. Maybe you'd like to take a photo. The view's kinda special.' They stood beside the vehicle and stared all about them. Occasionally the landscape was broken by trees but mainly it was vines, standing some five feet high and ripening, with an ultimate distant backdrop of the small reservoir, deep blue in the morning sunlight. Chambon started taking photographs, hoping to look as professional as possible and succeeding, just as he always did.

'Monterey County,' explained Coburn, 'has good soil but not what the French would call an ideal climate. So we've laid on our own water. From that reservoir there's a pipe, a big pipe, which brings the water to an entire complex of small ones, which in turn lead to a series of sprinklers, which spray every bit of the vineyard.'

'So you make your own rain?' exclaimed Emma.

'In California—we make everything. The only difference between us and God is that He only took six days.'

'That's the sort of quote I like,' said Emma.

Coburn looked skywards. 'Well, I sure hope that He does too. Anyway, what the hell! We're proud of what we've achieved. When we want it to rain, we press a button in the control house. It rains. When we want it to stop raining, we press the other button. We want to inject a little fertilizer into the ground? We just feed it into the pipeline and the water carries it along the spray system. A thousand acres can be sprayed, fertilized, protected in minutes. It's almost a one man job. Better still—if the ground's too dry, the sprinkler system can switch itself on. Anyway, let's get down among the vines.'

'And what type of grapes are these here?' enquired Fraser, as the Range-Rover cruised down the hill, through a low stone wall which seemed to be the perimeter and then into the central road, closely bounded by the vines.

'A lot of Chardonnay. They're goddamned bastards to grow but worth it. We're also producing Pinot Noir and some Cabernet Sauvignon, rapidly expanding in the red wines. It's a seller's market, if you've got the right product. Some of our earlier reds weren't so good. Gee! That's an admission. Will you print that?'

'You bet,' said Emma, laughing.

'I'd better be more careful what I say.' He gave her a smile to tell her that he was joking and what he really wanted was a couple of hours in the sack with her.

'And do you own all this yourself, Mr Coburn?' asked Fraser.

'Nope. I've got backers. Shareholders. And the loan I took in '74 for the refinancing.'

'Anyone interesting?' it was the start of the agreed strategy of loading the questions.

'Does that really matter?' Coburn looked at them for a moment, just slightly defensive. 'Oh, what the hell. They're various corporations.'

'Tax shelters, I suppose?' There was a sting to the observation, only slightly lessened by Fraser's tone of voice.

'Could be. The way they manage their tax affairs ain't

no problem of mine.'

'What about Great Pinewood Shores?'

Coburn slowed down and looked across at Fraser with renewed respect. 'You're well informed. They gave us the loan.'

'Not very difficult to establish,' said Fraser. 'Dun and Bradstreet.' One phone call to the famous company know-alls had instituted an immediate status search. The solicitor was about to continue with questions about McMac, about New Orleans, when his train of thought was interrupted as, all around them, it started to rain. 'That's incredible,' he said instead, as the entire sky was filled with the finest of rain, like a Scotch mist. The sprays had started to work. 'Who would have started that?' enquired Fraser.

Coburn looked puzzled. 'I guess the night-guard but I sure didn't expect that. He wouldn't turn it on with me coming. I guess the tensiometer must have activated. It's one of the best gadgets we've got. If the soil moisture tension is wrong, then it switches on the sprinklers. That way the vines get the best possible care. But I wasn't expecting it now. Anyway, we can keep on going down, take a look at the control unit and I'll show you how it works. You're gonna like it.'

The 'rain' continued to spatter the windscreen as they descended the valley at walking pace, stopping now and again for Coburn to point out matters of particular interest. But Fraser wanted to get back to his line of questioning. 'You Californians are doing pretty well with all this French trouble?'

'You're right. Our exports to Europe are up eight per cent — and that's a lot of bread. But those French — they sure do bring it on themselves, don't they? And the Germans now, with all this sugaring of the wine. A lot of gangsters they are.'

Fraser ignored the comment. 'Who does your PR work?'

'An agency down in L.A.'

'Not Karen Schunberg?' Fraser knew the answer, for Chambon's investigations on the stories all seemed to lead back to the one name.

Fraser looked hard at Coburn, who in turn looked at the road ahead. 'No. I don't know her. It sure ain't her.'

It was his first obvious lie and Fraser decided to try a bit of bluff. 'She said that she acted for you.'

'Then I guess she was mistaken.'

It was Emma's turn. 'You use Hyatt Hotels?'

'The Hyatt chain? Sure, I like them. Most everybody does. They're beautiful.'

'The one at Savannah? The one at Maui?'

'I guess so. Lots of places. Look, what is this? Do you want to know how many times a day I go to the john or do you want to know about my vines?'

Fraser was unabashed. 'Didn't you expect to do rather well out of the New Orleans wine auction recently?'

'Now look here, I don't understand your line of questioning but you take my advice—stick to the subject.'

'All right. Let's get straight to the point.' It was Chambon speaking now. 'You fixed up a warehouse in Sète from where you had wine switched, seeking to discredit the French.'

'Bullshit.' Coburn stopped the vehicle. 'Say! Who are you guys?' He unwound the window, more for something to do while he assessed the situation than for any other reason. Then his brow puckered and his nostrils twitched.

'What kind of fertilizer are you using?' enquired Fraser. 'It's got a curious smell.'

'I don't know neither. But it don't smell right.' Coburn jumped out on to the tarmac and the passengers did the same. Together they entered the vines, all the time sniffing the air. 'Shit!' Coburn turned and ran to the vehicle. 'Get in quick. Something's wrong down at the control unit.'

In contrast to the measured pace of the start of the journey, Coburn now drove with increasing speed, hurrying towards the reservoir. They crossed a ridge about half way down the valley and then a brick building, came into sight close to the reservoir. The four occupants took in the scene instantly, although each saw and recorded something different. Six giant fuel tankers with hoses like elephant's trunks were connected to the feeder pipe leading into the vines. Nearer the reservoir a man was doing something by the pipe which drew the water from the reservoir and into the system. Of the tanker drivers there was no sign. As the Range-Rover narrowed the gap towards the building, Fraser saw the body of a man lying on the ground, near one of two parked cars. Coburn saw it too and knew it to be the body of his employee, but there was no time to explain the position.

A common fear replaced antagonism. No one spoke. With only fifty yards till they were out of the green forest of vines, the first water from the reservoir was released by Ramalpo, flooding the sprinkler system, thundering through the network. Instantaneously, the world seemed to shake, to turn upside down, to be a searing, explosive mixture of red and black. At once the car was surrounded by flames and acrid black smoke. The tankers had been charged with benzine spirit, which Ramalpo had discharged throughout the system, followed by the lethal additive of potassium. The inlet specially provided for injection of fertilizers had proved invaluable as the benzine and potassium had been pumped, neat, until every inch of the vineyard had been thoroughly sprayed. The missing ingredient needed to trigger off an explosion was nothing more deadly than water, and when Ramalpo had opened the water supply from the reservoir, the fiery explosive had turned a thousand acres of vineyard into an immediate inferno. Every vine was on fire, every inch of ground, every acre, was now aflame as far as Ramalpo could see, and in the middle of it all was the Range-Rover, which by now was itself aflame from the lethal mixture which had settled on it.

'For God's sake get out!' shouted Fraser. 'We've got to run for it.' But even as he spoke, thick black smoke surrounded the vehicle, shrouding it in darkness. Daytime had become night. As he was speaking Fraser was opening the back door, dragging Emma with him into the blackness and facing the stinking, roaring heat from all around.

He glanced over his shoulder and was pleased to see that Henri was right behind. 'I'm with you, Barty,' came the reassuring answer. 'I can't get out of the front. The fire's too bad there.' Vaguely, but without any feeling of concern, Fraser saw Coburn scrambling through the vehicle towards safety. Breathing was difficult and so Fraser pulled Emma past the front of the vehicle and then forced her to the ground, where the tarmac was hot, sticky and melting. But the air was bearable. Rapidly they started to crawl towards safety.

Behind them, Henri Chambon was now out of the vehicle, Coburn at his side, but at that moment the Range-Rover's petrol tank exploded like a giant bomb. Chambon, the man whose courage and initiatives had been Fraser's prop, was killed instantly as a spear of fragmented metal pierced his brain. Coburn too received the full force of the explosion, which knocked him unconscious and hurled him bodily through the burning air until he was deposited into the central heat of the blazing vines.

'Henri?' screamed Fraser, hoping that his voice would be heard, but knowing that it would not. He waited for a moment. 'Stay here,' he commanded Emma. 'I'm going back to look for Henri. He should have been with us by now.' Emma lay there, stuck to the ground in the boiling temperatures. Moments later, Fraser was back. 'There's no point waiting for Henri,' he shouted. 'He won't be joining us.' Together, shuffling close to the ground in the eighteen inches or so of almost clear air, they progressed rapidly until they could see beyond the burning line of vines. There was the man who had operated the control valve, the man who had set free the inroad of water which the pumps had scattered to all quarters of the system.

From where he stood Ramalpo had been unaware that, unusually, Coburn had not been alone. He'd heard the explosion, had judged that Coburn could not have survived it, but preferred to wait, gun in hand, occasionally looking at his watch, only half expecting to see anything. He saw no one, for the couple were lying just far enough into the blaze to be shrouded by the smoke, and while the flames were dancing beside them and over their heads, they were safe and free from immediate death. But they couldn't stay there long. The scorching temperatures were nearly unbearable.

'You all right?' Fraser asked.

A grunted 'yes' was the best which Emma could manage. The white trouser-suit which she had worn for the interview was now blackened with tar and shredded, showing that she had been wearing very little underneath. Her long fair hair was singed and smeared with black, while her face was covered in a mixture of blood and tar.

'Plan A,' said Fraser, 'is to stay here as long as we can endure it. Whoever that bugger is out there, he'll only hang around till he's sure that Coburn's dead.'

'OK. But what's Plan B?' Her voice was faint. 'Open some champagne?'

'If he starts to come in this direction, then we have the advantage of surprise. He won't see us unless he gets down to ground level. When he's almost on us, you make a run for that orange Datsun. I expect that was the night watchman's. The other car, the big green one, will be his. If we're lucky there'll be keys in the Datsun. Don't run till I say so.' He was surprised to find the way that he'd taken control now that Henri was dead. 'As you run, I'll sort out the man. When I've done that, I'll join you in the car.' He turned his head sideways, patted her and gave her a smile of reassurance. 'Easy, isn't it? Good copy for you, too.'

She looked at him with a semblance of a smile. 'Yes.' But she looked unconvinced.

'Go away. Go away, you bastard!' That was still their best hope as they lay there in the intense heat, the air noisy and crackling. Emma's arm was sprawled across Fraser's shoulder and her beautifully manicured nails dug into his flesh with the pain which she was suffering. 'You're doing fine,' he reassured her. 'He's bound to go away soon.' But the man didn't, simply staring in a dispassionate manner, gun pointing downwards, his sallow face showing no emotion about the conflagration.

From the distance came the sound of further explosions. The reverberation shook the ground and Ramalpo looked at his watch and gave a nod of satisfaction. Right on time. The time bombs, planted during the night, had worked with precision, heralding the end of the bottling plant, the end of the storage tanks, the end of the fermentation plant and the end of the unit. The end of the Minstrel Creek Winery. The end for Coburn. Ramalpo permitted himself a smile. His mission was almost complete.

Through bloodshot eyes and with time passing seemingly not at all, Fraser at last got an inkling that the man was about to leave. Whereas before he'd been motionless, eyes staring at the windswept flames, now he was moving about, restless, eyes searching for any last hint of movement. Then the man's footsteps started to approach the road through the vines. 'Don't bend down, you bastard!' muttered Fraser.

With the man perhaps ten yards away, they were safe as the footsteps stopped and then turned away. Fraser could see the highly polished buckles on the black shoes, the neat, razor-sharp creases in the black trousers. Another five seconds and they would have been safe, but one of the wooden posts which had been supporting the sprinkler system collapsed and a piece of flaming timber fell across Emma's back. Her scream was instant and piercing, as her flesh was burnt. The receding footsteps stopped as the watcher was galvanized. Then they turned, starting to approach the fire once again. Even as he was watching, Fraser pushed aside the burning spar but the few seconds the wood had lain there had scarred Emma's back for life. 'Plan B. You *must* do it, Emma. Forget the pain — or you're dead.' The words, whispered in her ear from a few inches at first brought no interest but then she started to draw herself up, tears pouring from her eyes.

Still the footsteps drew nearer — ten yards, six, five and then three yards. Still the man did not bend down. Their advantage of surprise was on a fuse which was liable to blow out at any moment. Using his good leg for leverage, Fraser edged himself into a crouch and, like the first charge of a bull, sprang out of the smoky nowhere to collide with the man's midriff. Ramalpo grunted with pain as he was winded.

'Run. Run, Emma!' Though his thoughts were on the stranger in the black suit and white shirt, now lying on the ground, momentarily disadvantaged, he saw a response from his side. 'Run — and fast.' The force of the blow had made Ramalpo drop his gun but Fraser had no time to look for it before the man started to rise to his feet quicker than Fraser would have thought possible. The eyes were blackened with hatred as they searched around for the gun. Without it, the man felt naked. As Ramalpo raised himself from his knees, Fraser waited till he was on a point of balance and then swung his right leg like a punt for touch, so that his toe struck Ramalpo at the base of his nose. A second later would have been too late and the man would have grabbed his leg, but the timing had been good and Ramalpo's head rocked back and he fell sideways, tears rushing involuntarily to his eyes, blood pouring from his nose. Fraser debated whether to hit him again but decided against it, and instead hurried in the direction of the Datsun, glad of the sessions with Grunt Gordon. Lurching forward rather than running, he reached the Datsun just as Ramalpo rose from the ground.

'Quick, Barty, quick.' Emma was in the passenger seat and had cleverly thought to open the driver's door. 'The keys are in it.' As Fraser slammed the door he could see Ramalpo on his feet now, shaking his head and seeking reorientation.

On second pull the Datsun's engine fired and, after ramming the clutch into first gear, he set it rolling. 'We've got to get the hell out of here. We'll follow the road round the reservoir. We'll never get away up the road we came.'

'Who is he?'

'God knows. Some type of hit man.' The words were punctuated by gasps, caused as much by tension as by their previously smoky environment. 'Certainly no friend of ours—or of Coburn's, come to that. How's your back?'

'Agony. I'd give anything to dive into the reservoir.'

'At least you're alive. The Editor'll pay well for this. Keep you in champagne for a fortnight. What's happening behind us?'

Emma turned round, wincing at the pain as she did so. 'He's got his car moving. He's certainly following us. He's about three hundred yards back.'

'Three hundred yards! With us in this and him in that great big roadster?' The equation was obvious and Fraser fell silent as he pushed his foot as hard down as the little car would take.

'He's going to kill us, isn't he?'

'If he catches us—yes. He won't want any witnesses. So we've got to beat him. Somehow.'

As Fraser headed east, visibility ahead was fine. The clean fresh air from the reservoir on their left made high speeds safe and welcoming. But ahead there was a dog-leg in the valley and the reservoir followed the contours, as did the road, nipped between vineyard and water. As they drove, a wall of flame accompanied them down their right side for acre upon flaming acre. The sky all around was black with swirling benzine'd smoke which rose now to hundreds of feet and filled the distant horizon.

'We'll have to go through that. Look.' Fraser pointed ahead as they rounded the bend in the reservoir. They could see that the single track road disappeared into thick black smoke for a distance of perhaps two hundred yards. Beyond that, as the road changed direction again, visibility was clear.

'He's about two hundred yards behind us now.' Emma's voice was urgent.

'In that case he'll catch us before we reach any major road. We're on our own.'

'You're sure he's gaining still?'

' 'Course I'm bloody sure. He's going like a dingbat.'

Fraser hunched himself over the wheel, urging the car forward. 'OK. When we get to the smoke do what I say. No questions. It'll be dangerous.' He stared ahead at the smoke which he could see now was flecked with orange and red wisps of flame, dancing to a height of perhaps thirty feet. 'Open your door now. Just a fraction.' As he spoke the wall of fiery smoke was sixty yards away. 'Right. As soon as we get into the smoke, I'll slow down. Get out. Close the door. Roll straight down the embankment and into the reservoir. He won't see you and you won't get burnt. Or, if you do, the water'll put out the flames straight away.' She was about to respond but there wasn't time before the thick smoke enveloped the car. Instantly he dropped speed to walking pace and she flung herself out. As she disappeared from view, he heard screams of anguish as she was caught in the fiery heat into which he'd cast her.

He drove on for another fifty yards and then spun the car until it was broadside across the road. Time to get out! And quick! Inside the car all was blackness. Outside all was blackness, save for the occasional lick of menacing flame and the roar of a thousand acre fire. The Datsun's paint was blistering and pungent.

Christ! How do these bloody doors open! Where's the handle? Soon the le Baron would be upon him. Good! That's it! Hell! No, it's not! It's the window winder. Oh Christ! What's this? Pull up? Push down? Christ — the heat! He'll hit me. Oh God!

Ramalpo, pushing the le Baron to the limit, entered the smoke without easing his speed at all, headlights on, engine roaring, obsessed with elimination.

Thank God! That's it! The door opened and he was out and, for a second, standing by the car. From the darkness appeared the glare of four lights bearing down on him. With no time to think, Fraser threw himself towards the embankment and was still in the air as Ramalpo's limousine struck the side of the Datsun at full bore, tossing the small car high into the air and down on to its roof. Ramalpo's head struck his windscreen with atrocious force, his chest being crushed beyond recognition by the penetration of the steering-column. Multiple fractures of the skull and a ruptured aorta gave him no chance of survival. Death was immediate.

After the impact Fraser's thoughts were hazy in his roly-poly confusion from the fall down the embankment. By the water's edge there was no smoke and he lay still, his left thigh throbbing and thumping out menacing

warnings about abuse. Yet he was alive and probably
safe. He could smell the burning paintwork of the two
cars, could imagine Ramalpo, shattered and burning in
the driving seat. It was a not unpleasing thought.
Overhead, the petrol tanks exploded while he cowered in
safety. Then he moved, balancing with all the grace of a
new-born foal, for somewhere not far away was Emma.
She had to be found.

Half crawling, half dragging himself through the
tangle of weeds and stunted bushes, at last he saw her,
lying like a broken doll, her head by a boulder, her eyes
shut and her body contorted. On her right temple there
was a gash and blood was flowing profusely. He twisted
himself round to look, to learn if there were any life in
her, for she seemed horribly still and deathly pale, apart
from the blood from the wound to her head. Feverishly he
felt for her wrist, seeking a pulse, and placed his other
hand below the remains of her white jacket to seek a
heartbeat. But such was the pounding of his own heart
that it was all too confusing. Yet surely she was alive.
Surely her breasts were rising and falling. Yes, they were.
Surely they were. Almost imperceptible. But surely they
were. For how long he waited without daring to move he
would never know. Time had no meaning. But it must
have been five minutes before her head stirred and her
eyes opened, their expression blank, disorder behind
them.

'Emma. Emma! Thank God!' He bent forward and
kissed her and was rewarded with a smile as the California
which Emma was seeing became clearer.

She could feel his hand on her chest, could see his face
close to hers, anxious and concerned. 'Barty! At a time
like this! Get your hand out at once.' He did, but only so
that he could cradle her head in both hands while he
kissed her again.

'Don't move. I'll put a handkerchief over that bump on

your head. I want the bleeding to stop.'

'Where is he? Where's that man?'

'Not watching us—that's for sure.' Fraser looked around him. 'Dead for certain.' He kissed her, looking deep into her eyes. 'I ought to go and find help. We'll need to get you to hospital but I can't leave you—not yet anyway.'

'No, don't leave me, Barty. Not if that man might still be alive. I'm too frightened for that. Let's just lie here till we're rescued. But no more hanky-panky.' She pulled the remnants of her jacket across. 'You ought to be ashamed of yourself. A man of your age trying to take advantage of me while I'm unconscious. You're the sort we write about in the *Daily Topic*.'

# SAN FRANCISCO

Emma lay in her hospital bed, pleased with her 'piece'. It should be just about comprehensible to the discerning readers of the *Daily Topic*. If they didn't understand, the Editor could always put out a strip cartoon version the following week.

'Read it, Barty. See what you think.' Bandaged round her head, bandaged round her shoulders, she was not looking her best.

'Mind if I eat your grapes?' he enquired. 'It seems appropriate. I'll read at the same time.'

He flicked through the pages, all the while absent-mindedly picking off her grapes until at last he looked up. 'You've given them all the sex and violence and none of the real facts.'

'You don't bore *Daily Topic* readers with *facts*! Not unless they're bare. It just makes them turn over to the titties on the next page.'

'So you're not going to tell them that Coburn had twisted Mocari into thinking that the plan was just to sink the French? I mean, aren't you going to tell them that Coburn's real interest was to kill off the loan-sharking subsidiary of Great Pinewood Shores, Inc., and the wealth of the parent company?'

'Much too complicated. Mention the word "sharks" and my readers think of *Jaws*. Those that can count might think of *Jaws 2*.' She was trying to laugh behind her bandage. 'By the way, what is a loan-shark?'

'Well, you remember Coburn told us of the collapse of the trade in 1974. That's when he borrowed money but then the income didn't service the capital borrowed and so, in desperation, he borrowed from a subsidiary of Great Pinewood Shores. The parent company is apparently reputable, with vineyards in France, but the reality is that the whole outfit was a bunch of gun-toting hoods. So anyway, Coburn got his re-financing but Spiggola's loan-sharks manipulated the small print, upped the interest rates, turned the screw, piled interest on interest, so that Coburn could never get out of debt. And his shareholders got edgy.'

'I can nearly understand.'

'Coburn's vineyard was backed by shareholders and with Spiggola's loan-sharks creaming off the profit, they got restless, particularly when none other than Great Pinewood Shores made them an offer for their shares.' Fraser grinned in approval at the deviousness of it all. 'The shareholders had given Coburn two years to get into profit but he could see that profit was impossible. Spiggola saw to that. From papers in Coburn's safe we know that he'd discovered the link between the loan-sharks and Great Pinewood Shores, so he decided to kick them where it hurt. Right up their Wall Street Quotation! Undermine their assets, neuter their buying power. But he was too clever to attack their French vineyard alone.

He attacked the whole French market so that the shares fell on Wall Street and the assets were written down. In the meantime his own turnover would rise and there was no way that his shareholders would want to sell.'

'But what about the wine in France?'

'Once confidence returned, Coburn was sitting on a warehouse full of the best wines in the world, ready to sell at huge profits. But for Henri, he'd have got away with it.'

'But how many deaths have there been? That's what my readers like to know.'

'At least eleven.'

'Hmm! We'll call it over twenty. It sounds better. What about Mocari? Was he tortured?'

'Enough of that, Emma! Anyway I've got some other news for you. Le Breton & Co. have sent me a cable. They've offered me the position of Chairman.'

'You! A Chairman! Too much drinking port in that job. You'll rot your *good* leg. Then where will you be?'

'Any port in a storm.' His groan came before hers.

'But please, Barty—don't give in to Bream. Joining le Breton & Co. is the easy way out.'

'Don't worry. I've no intention of giving in to Bream. I can still be a solicitor and Chairman. It's all a bit complicated but *my solicitors* have unearthed the minutes of the Partners Meeting when I got the boot.'

'And?'

'The combined brains of Anderson, fresh from the poop deck, and David Bream, from Royal Ascot, couldn't even fix the minutes.'

'You've lost me.'

'The minutes show that the Partners were *unanimous* in their decision as the result of intense *persuasion* by dear old David. Not that I can imagine him persuading *anybody* about *anything*.'

'Does that help?'

'And how! It only means that their decision was unlawful. If they'd all been agreed from the start to expel me, without giving me a chance to be heard, then I'd have had no legal rights. But as he had to *persuade* them, I'm in business. I was entitled to be heard at the meeting. I've won. They'll have to settle. Pay my costs too.' Fraser turned serious. 'Do you see me as a Chairman . . . Chairman of a reputable company by Royal Appointment?'

'With this bandage round my head, I can't see anything. Stop daydreaming, you old buffer, and pour the champagne.'